ACCLAIM FOR

# THE STENCH OF HONOLULU

"I recently humiliated myself in the prestigious Pump Room restaurant by laughing out loud, to the point of tears, while reading THE STENCH OF HONOLULU. Jack Handey is the funniest writer in America. And his funny is a very particular, sublime kind of funny—it builds and builds and is related to his supreme control of language. It is witty, minimal, subversive, and also strangely sweet. Read this book, and you will feel better, period."

—George Saunders, *New York Times* bestselling author of *Tenth of December,* to the *New York Post*

"A well-oiled laugh-machine. A prose cartoon...a book that glimmers like an oasis of funny in the desert of snark that surrounds us." —*Paste Magazine*

# THE STENCH OF HONOLULU

# THE STENCH
*of*
# HONOLULU

*A Tropical Adventure*

## JACK HANDEY

**GRAND CENTRAL**
**PUBLISHING**

NEW YORK   BOSTON

Copyright © 2013 by Jack Handey
Illustrations copyright © 2013 by Jim Cook

Grand Central Publishing
Hachette Book Group
1290 Avenue of the Americas
New York, NY 10104

www.HachetteBookGroup.com

Printed in the United States of America


Originally published in hardcover by Hachette Book Group
First trade edition: July 2015
10 9 8 7 6 5 4 3 2 1

Grand Central Publishing is a division of
Hachette Book Group, Inc.
The Grand Central Publishing name and logo are
trademarks of Hachette Book Group, Inc.

The Hachette Speakers Bureau provides a wide range of
authors for speaking events. To find out more, go to
www.hachettespeakersbureau.com or call (866) 376-6591.

The publisher is not responsible for websites (or their content)
that are not owned by the publisher.

Library of Congress Cataloging-in-Publication Data
Handey, Jack, 1949-
The stench of Honolulu / Jack Handey.—1st ed.
p. cm.
ISBN 978-1-4555-2238-5 (hardcover)—ISBN 978-1-4555-2239-2
(ebook)—ISBN 978-1-61969-360-9 (audiobook)  1. Travel—
Fiction.  2. Honolulu (Hawaii)—Fiction.  I. Title.
PS3608.A712S74 2013
813'.6—dc23                    2012032114

ISBN 978-1-4555-3453-1 (pbk.)

To Bill Novak

# THE STENCH OF
# HONOLULU

## Don's Offer

WHEN MY friend Don suggested we go on a trip to the South Seas together, and offered to pay for the whole thing, I thought, Fine, but what's in it for me?

After he explained that I'd be getting a free vacation, I still hesitated. It was true that, jobwise, I had some time. I had just been fired again. And after working there for nearly two months, I was ready for a vacation.

But finally I said no. For one thing, I don't really like the tropics. The last time I went to the Caribbean I wound up in a bongo factory, forced to make bongos.

Also, I was making good progress on my

novel, *Muscular Angry Clown*. It's about a well-built circus clown with a hot temper. I was at the part where he breaks the neck of the evil lion tamer.

Also, I had been dating this woman, and we were really being in love. I can't remember her name right now, but she's great.

I knew Don would ask me again. He doesn't have a lot of good friends. That's because he doesn't hang around in bars a lot, like I do. That's where you make your really good friends, in bars. Don spends most of his time at work. He's a counselor for deranged children.

Sure enough, Don called again. He said the reason for the trip was that his divorce had become final, and he wanted to go someplace far away. And he wanted me to go because he had a bunch of different emotions, and he wanted someone to share them with.

That was when I pretended something was wrong with the phone and hung up. When Don called back I used my Chinese voice and said, "He no here!"

Why, then, you're wondering, did I call Don back and agree to go on the trip with him? Someone lit a fire under me. And that someone was Conk and Conky Pingle. They dragged me into an alley and lit a fire under me. They said that if I didn't pay them the money I owed them, they would put a device on my head.

"What kind of device?" I said.

Not a device, they said, a *vise*.

South Seas, here I come!

# Warnings

AFTER I agreed to go, there were ominous warning signs:

I got a letter addressed to "Occupant." But someone had crossed it out and written "Resident."

I saw my name in a bowl of spaghetti, misspelled.

I spotted a quarter on some steps. But when I tried to pick it up, it was stuck down with bubble gum. Then I heard the sound of pixies laughing.

A burglar broke into my apartment while I was out. He didn't take anything, but he left an angry note.

I went to check on the new sidewalk.

It was smooth again. There was no sign anywhere of my footprints, my handprints, or my face print. It was as if I had never existed.

A squirrel stared at me. I looked away, but when I looked back he was still staring.

I dreamed I was in the jungle, holding a lighted stick of dynamite. I tried to throw it, but it stuck to my hand. Then I noticed the brand name: Sticky Dynamite. I woke up in a cold sweat.

Scariest of all was the hideous old crone. She pointed her long, crooked finger at Don and me and croaked, "Do not go on this trip. There is nothing but death and destruction." Then she said, "But if you do go, I can get you a really good deal." And she did. All we had to do was connect through St. Louis.

# The Gift

WE HAD our plane tickets and were almost out the door when the crone said, "Wait, I want to give you two handsome men something very special." She lowered the blinds and flipped the sign to Closed. She led us to a darkened room in the back and lit a candle. "What I am about to give you is very old but very precious." Uh-oh.

She opened a creaky cabinet, tearing several spiderwebs apart. I felt sorry for the spiders and all the work they had done. She took out a folder and blew the dust off. After we finished coughing, she blew some more dust, and we coughed again. Then she put the folder back and took out something else.

"I am among the last of my kind. Soon there will be no more travel agents. I want someone to have this before it's too late." She spread out a ragged, faded map. It showed a large, mysterious island in the middle of the ocean, a land that I had never heard of. Then it hit me: This was the same place Don had mentioned. And the same place our tickets were to. It was all starting to fit together.

The crone tapped her clawlike fingernail on a spot deep in the jungle. "This is where you will find it. The greatest treasure known to man. The Golden Monkey!" She cackled a screeching cackle.

I started to ask her a question, but she let out another screeching cackle. When she finally stopped I said, "Why don't you go find the Golden Monkey yourself?" I was smirking, because it was such a good question.

She said, "I am too old. Soon I will be—"

"Dead?"

"Retired," she said.

I kissed her on the cheek. Don claims I made out with her, but Don's a liar.

# The Bible

WHEN YOU have a real treasure map in your hand, all sorts of thoughts go through your head. The first is, Don't lose the map. The second is, Hey, what happened to the map? The third is, Oh, yeah, I gave it to Don. The fourth is, Hey, where'd Don go? The fifth is, Oh, there he is.

Don made me swear on the Bible to keep the whole thing secret. I went and got my Bible. Inside I had carved out the shape of a gun in the pages. That's because if I ever get a gun, I'm going to hide it in there. If I'm at home when a burglar breaks in, I'll say something like "Is it okay if I read my Bible while you're robbing me?" Who's going to say no? That would be crazy. And then I'll open the Bible to the Ten Commandments and say, "Thou shalt not..." And when the burglar says, "Thou shalt not what?" I'll pull out the gun and kill him.

With the Pingle brothers after me, I was anxious to get going. "Let's get over there and steal the thing," I said. Don said it wouldn't really be stealing because the civilization that made the Golden Monkey was probably long gone. Come on, Don, it's stealing. To prove it I opened my Bible to that part, but it had been carved out.

# Uncle Lou

I DECIDED to get some advice from Uncle Lou. He'd found all sorts of golden things over the years.

His servant led me down the wide hallway, past the glass case holding his old boxing gloves and championship belt, and into the library.

"God says we shouldn't crave gold," said Uncle Lou, puffing on his cigar. "But that's easy for Him to say. His whole throne is made out of it."

He pointed to a golden iguana on the mantel. "I betrayed my entire expedition to get this," he said. He pointed to a golden mouse. "I pushed a man off a cliff to get this one." He pointed to a little golden snail. "This one I got at a flea market."

I told Uncle Lou only that we were going after something goldish and monkey-ish. He got a faraway look in his eyes, I think from all the pills he was taking. "A golden monkey, eh?" he said. I didn't answer, just nodded, so as not to break my oath. "And you know where it is?" he said. I just did a tiny nod.

I got worried Uncle Lou might want to come with us, along with his little dog Screwball. But fortunately he was too ill. His Tomlin's gland was giving out. It might even go spastic. His treasure-hunting days were over.

He urged me to go. "This trip might finally turn you into a man," he said, which made my eyes well up and my lip quiver.

He stirred himself another bourbon and Coke and finally handed me a glass of wine. It had a familiar powdery taste that I couldn't quite place.

He jabbed his cigar at me. "Always remember this: If your friend falls in quicksand, offer to throw him a rope. But first get him to throw you his wallet."

"Ahh, I see," I said. "But what if he wants to see the rope first?"

"You're missing the point."

"Maybe you could just show him a vine and say it's a rope."

"You don't need to show him anything."

"Maybe you could say you need the wallet to go buy a rope."

I felt woozy. I toppled over. The last thing I remember was Screwball pulling off my glasses and chewing on them.

The next day it felt like I had been run over by a bicycle, which I had, as I staggered home from Uncle Lou's. My head hurt. My body hurt. I even had a sore tooth. The trouble with going to Uncle Lou's was he was always drugging you. I guess he thought it was funny. Yes, the food was good, but half the time you didn't even remember it.

One day I would get my revenge. My plan

was to get a metal container and fill it with sizzling acid and go to his house. If everything worked correctly, the acid would eat through the container after I had already left, and spill out onto the table, and ruin it, and Uncle Lou would have to buy a new one.

# The Flight

I ASKED Don if we were taking any Sticky Dynamite on the trip, and he said no. That was a relief. How about hand grenades? No again. That was a disappointment. I'd like to throw a hand grenade sometime. Imagine pulling the pin out, throwing the grenade at something, and watching whatever you threw it at blow up. Maybe I'll get to do that in Heaven.

The airplane flight was long and boring. The only interesting part was a magazine article I read on the way, about dandelions. It said that not everything that looks like a dandelion actually *is* a dandelion—even if it blows like a dandelion. It could be a "false dandelion." I thought that was pretty interesting.

I also read a card that showed me how to open the exit door next to my seat. Yeah, like I'd ever want to do that.

The great thing about sitting next to a stranger on an airplane is you can ask him all sorts of questions. "What's a good nickname for me?" I asked, explaining I had narrowed it down to "Biff," "Wrong Way," and "Studs." He didn't seem to have a preference.

As I sat there slurping on my straw,

trying to decide, I said, "Wait a minute! What about 'Slurps'?" He looked like he was in pain. I don't blame him—it was a tough one. I went over it in my mind, out loud. I decided I liked "Slurps" better than "Biff" or "Studs," but not better than "Wrong Way." Then it hit me: how about "Wrong Way Slurps"!

I turned to the stranger, and that was when I got an idea for an even better nickname: "The Sleep Pretender."

# *Honolulu*

BY THE time we started to land, I had changed my nickname back to "Wrong Way Slurps." It just hits the ear better.

We came in low over the jungle. It looked so peaceful, except for the volcano shooting boulders into the air and the monkeys fighting each other in the treetops. So this was the mysterious land of "Hawaii."

We landed in a dirty, coastal backwater called Honolulu. The stench was unbearable. Honolulu once had a thriving fishing industry, but now the only thing left was the stench. The coral reef, it turns out, is actually thousands of old fish heads. Honolulu is also home to the Happy Baby Stink Bomb

Factory—the largest in the world—which adds to the stench. Also, the town is infested with thousands of belchwood trees.

When we got off the plane the smell hit us full in the face. A scary-looking transvestite put flower necklaces around our necks and said, "Aloha." Someone told me later that *aloha* is a curse word.

As we walked through town we held our noses, which marked us as tourists. Pushy street vendors tried to sell us nose plugs, but I'd read it's better to get your nose plugs at your hotel.

Thugs and lowlifes glared at us from every rotting, ramshackle street corner. Prostitutes beckoned from every window or wrestled each other in the muddy streets. A dead bum was being eaten by vultures. Another bum held up a sign, See My Friend Get Eaten By Vultures—2 Paleekas.

Honolulu seemed like a good place to get Shanghaied or Hong Konged or Bangkoked. One thing for sure, it was no vacation town.

\*　　\*　　\*

We came to the town square. In the center was a big bronze statue of the discoverer of Hawaii, Sir Edmund Honolulu III. He was holding up one hand in greeting and pinching his nose with the other. I guess the place smelled even then. The plaque, from the People of Hawaii, said:

HE GREAT MAN.
HE FIND US.

# Coca-Cola

WE WERE staying at the best hotel in town, the Coca-Cola Hotel. It was called that because the owner had found a Coca-Cola sign on the beach and used it as his hotel sign. Which he hung from a rusty chain he also found. Man, that guy's lucky. I never find anything on the beach.

The owner was a giant grizzly of a man, with long, grizzled hair and wild, frizzy sideburns. He had a grisly scar that had been drizzled across his face. Just to look up at him made you dizzy. His name was Bizzy.

We found him in the hotel courtyard, shooting a crossbow at a big target. The target was the outline of a man running away, looking back over his shoulder in panic.

"You Bizzy?" said Don.

"Bizzy not here," he replied.

When I pointed out that his name tag said "Hi, My Name Is Bizzy," he grinned. "You very smart. You must be tourist."

I started to tell him about my country, with its "cars" and "buildings," but he didn't seem interested. We followed him to the counter inside.

"Two room, fifty paleekas," Bizzy growled.

*"Fifty paleekas?!"* I said. I didn't know how much a paleeka was, but I think you're supposed to be outraged whenever somebody tells you how much something costs. Bizzy refused to bargain over the price, so I tried bargaining with Don, but he wouldn't bargain, either. So we settled at fifty paleekas, which seemed fair.


Bizzy was confused by my request for nose plugs. "You know, nose plugs," I said, pointing up my nostrils with two fingers. He jerked open a drawer full of clutter, fished around, and pulled out two old whiskey corks. "Those won't fit," I explained.

"Maybe I make them fit," he said with a weird smile. I guess he meant he would have to carve them down, so they would be smaller and fit comfortably.

Bizzy mumbled something to us as we headed up to our rooms.

"Sorry?" said Don.

*"Welcome Hawaii,"* he snarled impatiently.

As we climbed the stairs, Don gave me a Don look. And it wasn't because part of the bannister broke off in my hand. He said I shouldn't have told Bizzy that pretty soon we'd be paying in golden monkeys instead of paleekas.

I said, "Do you really think a guy who owns the whole Coca-Cola Hotel and can afford to have all his teeth sharpened, cares anything about golden monkeys?" *Think, Don.*

Once in my room, I took the treasure map from Don and laid it lightly on the table. The table instantly collapsed. I picked up one of the rotten table legs. "Hey, Don, look, Superman." I crushed it in my hand. I guess I shouldn't have done that, because the wood released a smell that was ten times worse than the normal town stench. Don and I covered our faces and staggered to the window. Every step we took broke through the floorboards, releasing more stench. We moved in slow, stinking motion.

We finally got the window open. Don took a deep breath, and threw up on the ground below. A mangy dog came by and ate the vomit, then emitted a gas so foul that we had to close the window.

Then we passed out.

# *Supplies*

BY THE next day, things had improved. My fingers were still swollen from the window slamming down on them, but getting better. So was my paper cut. And my tarantula bite.

The morning stench had lifted, and the afternoon stench had yet to set in. From my window I could see all the way across the bay to the town of Diarroa. The people of Diarroa, I was to learn, are stuck up. For them, nothing is better than living in Diarroa.

Don gave me a list of supplies to buy and some money. I finally got a look at a paleeka. It has a picture of the aging Queen of England in one corner and a shrunken head in the other. In the center is a picture of Sir Edmund Honolulu being roasted on a spit. In the background some natives are pointing at him and laughing.

I found Bizzy in the courtyard, installing broken pieces of glass into the wet cement atop the wall. The tips were all pointing up.

"It looks a lot prettier with those decorations," I offered. He didn't say anything. I guess he was concentrating.

Finally, he spoke. "You know," he said, testing the sharpness of a glass shard with his fingertip, "many seek Golden Monkey. All come back disappointed. I know many things Hawaii. Maybe you let me help you find what you seek."

I nodded, as if I had any idea what he was talking about. When people say things, usually it's best to nod or laugh. Sometimes you can laugh and then nod, but that can get tricky.

Bizzy led me to the lobby and picked out several brochures for me from the rack. I

25

started to ask him if he had finished my nose plugs yet. But I thought, No, be patient; Bizzy will let you know when he's done.

I adjusted the clothespin on my nose and, with the confidence of the sophisticated traveler, strutted off to explore the sights.

# The Sights

THERE WERE basically two bars in Honolulu. One was called Pops'. Coincidentally, it was owned by a guy named Pops. He was a big, friendly, ruddy-faced fellow, always ready with a joke and a hearty laugh. Which was why I got out of there right away. I went to the other bar, called Shut Up.

I had a couple of Drowsy Lifeguards, which is the local cocktail. I struck up a conversation with an old one-eyed man. I told him I noticed that he only had one eye. "You're very observant," he said. His other eye had been clawed out by that hawk that lives in Central Park in New York. "Oh, but everyone loves that hawk," he said bitterly.

He gave me a warning. He said we would never reach the Golden Monkey. In fact, we would not even get out of town. In fact, I wouldn't even get out of the bar. That was when I saw he had taped my wrist to my chair. In alarm I started swinging it around, knocking over bowls of dried geckos. The bartender threw me out. When I looked back, the one-eyed man was inviting someone else to sit with him, and getting his tape ready.

I made my way through the foul, steaming backstreets of Honolulu, dodging fistfights and buckets of slop thrown from windows. A boy carrying a wooden box called out, "Blacken your teeth, mister?"

I passed the Happy Baby Stink Bomb Factory, with its famous logo of a baby petting a skunk. The company motto, in quotes, read: "The Stink Bomb for the Common Man."

I noticed I was being followed. It turned out to be someone from the hotel. I thought that was nice. Wherever Don and I went, Bizzy sent someone to follow us.

The Stench of Honolulu

The brochures all said to go to the Honolulu Museum, and I don't like to disobey brochures. One exhibit explained how stench rot, over time, can corrode the strongest of wood. And even your bones.

Another exhibit had an interactive display that showed what you'd look like with the plague. It was pretty funny.

My favorite exhibit told how Hawaii was formed. Millions of years ago, under a soft blanket of warm blue ocean, two rock formations, lying side by side, began pushing and grinding against each other. Slowly at first, then harder and harder. The pushing and thrusting and grinding produced enormous quantities of heat and lava. Finally, when it seemed like the two formations could not take it any longer, the lighter one slid on top of the heavier one, and rode on top.

After the museum, I went to the so-called "beach," where you can hire a boat to take you out and harpoon a whale. Then the whale pulls you around while you hold on to a parachute. They said the harpoon doesn't really hurt the whale.

Some surfers were surfing in the murky, bad-smelling water. Most of them had severe skin lesions.

For me, the best part of Honolulu was Appliance Town. You can walk on a boardwalk that's built on top of all the old appliances that people have dumped. Fruit stands sold pieces of what they called "pineapple." It tasted so strange and foreign. I wish I could describe it to you.

I tried my luck at the Dynamite Throw, where you can throw lighted sticks of dynamite at cars that have washed ashore. My aim was off because of the sticky pineapple juice on my hands. I sent some people running.

I asked if they had any hand grenades to throw. They said grenades weren't allowed. I guess the explosives laws in Hawaii are pretty strict.

# The Souvenir

I WANDERED down a crooked back alley and came to a souvenir shop. I don't think I would have even noticed it except for a big neon sign that said, Souvenirs! Curios!

The shop had the usual tourist junk. But something caught my eye. I had never seen anything so exquisite. It was a little statue of a native girl with her arms held out. It was locked in a display case. I jimmied the lock with a paper clip and took it out.

"Be careful with that!" said the nervous shop owner, rushing over and grabbing it.

"Is it glass?" I said.

"No, something very rare."

"Rarer than glass?" I said.

"It's made out of stenchite, the solid form of stench. It is the pure, crystalline essence of stench." He said it was thousands of times more powerful than regular stench. Boy, how many times have you heard that?

Through some sort of complex mechanism I still don't understand, the statue did a dance called the "hula" when you tapped her. She was hypnotizing, and not in a way that makes you quit smoking. I had to have her.

"You have good taste," said the owner. But when I saw the price, I was stunned. "Is that paleekas or pipsqueakas?" I said, not really knowing what I meant. He said it was paleekas. I gritted my teeth and said okay. "What?" he said. I ungritted my teeth and said okay.

While he wrapped the hula girl in bubble wrap, I noticed something else: a wooden back scratcher! I had to have it! Instead of the hula girl!

"No, I think you should stick with the hula girl," he said.

"Yeah, you're right."

As he handed me the hula girl he told me that I must never ever let the hula girl touch something—I can't remember what it was—or it would set off a devastating chain reaction of utter destruction. Something like that.

I shrugged and turned to leave. He stopped me. "I don't think you're listening to me," he said. *"DO NOT LET THE HULA GIRL TOUCH* [whatever it was]. *IT WILL CAUSE A CATASTROPHE."*

I nodded and set off down the alley. The souvenir man called after me from his doorway. Something about wood.

# *Angry Don*

ON MY way back, I made some other stops. When I finally got to the hotel, Don was waiting. He had a frowning look of disapproval that I call "Don Maximus."

He started asking me all sorts of questions about the supplies. What kind did I get? How much did they cost? On and on.

Finally I had to confess I got mixed up and spent most of the money on prostitutes. He was furious. He said it was like I had robbed him.

"Maybe," I said, "but the prostitutes robbed *me*."

I started to tell him about the little stenchite hula girl, but then I thought, in the mood he's in, he probably wouldn't even like that.

Before he stormed off, Don told me to meet him at the wharf on Friday or he would head upriver without me. Oh, great, now I'm supposed to know what day of the week it is.

Don was really starting to make me mad. But I decided to channel my anger. And by channeling, I mean combining it with drinking.

The delivery boy arrived at my room with the case of scotch and some Hawaiian cigarettes. Scotch and cigarettes are "supplies," aren't they?

At least it was good scotch. Usually I can't afford Glenriddance, or even the cheaper version, Glencockie. But when you're spending paleekas, it's like it's not even real money.

I sucked on a Manatee and blew a couple of smoke rings across the room. I poured myself a large scotch. Maybe I wouldn't go upriver after all. Maybe Honolulu wasn't so bad.

There was a knock at the door. It was

the prostitute I had ordered, the one with epilepsy. (She was cheaper.) By then I had decided: I didn't need a solid-gold monkey. I had something more important: my integrity.

# *Reality*

THE NEXT morning things were looking shaky. And I don't just mean the prostitute. I was broke.

I thought about going on welfare, but I was too proud for that. So instead I became a street beggar. But good luck trying to compete with lepers and amputees, let alone starving orphans.

As I got more desperate, I even considered wiring the Pingle brothers for another loan, but the transpacific cable was down again. It's always getting chewed on by sea beavers.

There's no denying reality. I did once, and I wound up running across a field with my pants on fire, with an old man with a shotgun chasing me.

And the awful reality was, I needed a job.

I got hired right away herding crabs down on the "beach." (The signs always put quotes around *beach*; I think it's a legal thing.) Crab herding is a lot harder than it looks. You think that if a crab wanders off, and you go to get him, the other crabs will just stay put. Man, think again. Every night I came back to the hotel tired and "crabby," as they say in the business.

I got fired. I blame my supervisor, Oswaldo. Instead of teaching me good crab-herding skills, he was usually off watching two crabs fight to the death for his pleasure. Somehow it amused his twisted mind. I vowed that one day Oswaldo would be fighting to the death for *my* pleasure.

Don didn't leave on Friday. Bizzy kept talking him into getting more and more supplies. Don had supplies coming out the pachooga.

\*  \*  \*

Don and I avoided each other. One time we were passing each other in the hotel hallway. We didn't say a word, but as Don went by, I grabbed the treasure map from his back pocket. "Half of this is mine!" I said. I tried to tear it in half, but those old maps are really strong. Finally I was able to tear off part of it.

# Shattered Dreams

I APPLIED for some other jobs, if the form wasn't too long and I could get the pen chain untangled. But wherever I went they always asked the same question: "Do you have any crab-herding experience?" Try explaining to someone that you were fired from crab herding but it wasn't your fault. Besides, I'm not applying for a crab-herding job! Can't you get that through your head?!

I sank lower and lower. One night I took a powerful Hawaiian drug called paloomba. The next morning I found myself lying in a backyard with a big-armed woman yelling at me. Hey, quit yelling! I'm high on drugs, I'm not deaf!

I sank to a new low; it wasn't easy. There was a void in my life that had not been there before. Hungry and depressed, I wandered along the shimmering waters of the Bay of Diarroa, where children were playing with sailboats.

As I dragged myself back to the hotel, I passed the statue of Sir Edmund Honolulu. A bum with a blowtorch was cutting on it. "Hey, buddy, wanna buy a metal arm?" he said. Sure I would, but with what?

I had dreams once. Once I wanted to build the world's longest suspension bridge. But then I found out someone else had already done it.

Once I dreamed of becoming an astronaut, but they told me I needed some "training." Oh, well, let's all go get some "training." What a perfect world that would be.

Once I dreamed of putting an end to all fighting—except between women, for entertainment purposes.

I've always wanted to be an inventor. But the "powers that be" have decided the world doesn't need things like the cardboard canoe, for when you only feel like canoeing for an hour or so and you're too lazy to drag your canoe out of the water.

For a while I wanted to become a naturalist, until I found out it wasn't what I thought. They wear clothes.

I had dreams of starting a big family. Every night the children would gather in the parlor and play their musical instruments. Then I would announce who was the best and who was the worst.

I even imagined building a gigantic robot that would conquer the world. And so people wouldn't be mad, I would make the robot solar-powered.

One by one my dreams had been dashed against the wall like helpless coconuts.

## *No Way Out*

I KNEW what I had to do. It was all so clear. There was no other way. My whole life had been leading up to it. I left a note for Don, telling him I would probably never see him again.

I went to the top floor of the tallest building in Honolulu. A balcony ran the length of it. I paced back and forth, trying to get up the courage to open the door. The sign on the door said, Recruiting Office—Hawaiian Army.

I looked down at the street four stories below. I grew wobbly from the height and grabbed on to the railing. I swung my knee up onto it, to steady myself.

"Don't do it!" cried Don, suddenly behind me. He approached me warily. "This is not the answer. Don't throw your life away."

"I've thought it over, and this is the best solution."

"Life is too precious for this."

"But what about the benefits?"

"What benefits?" said Don.

"No more worries about food or shelter or any of that."

"Yes, but is it worth it?" He looked over the side. "You might get lucky and die. But what if you don't? Think of all the terror and pain and suffering."

Wow, was the Hawaiian Army really that bad?

Don was right next to me. He pulled out the treasure map and opened it. "This map is no good like this," he said. "It's missing a vital piece." He looked me in the eye.

I pulled out my little corner of the map. I took out my Mini Swingline Pocket Stapler, which I always carry, and carefully removed it from its holster. With about twenty-five fast, fist-pounding staples, I connected the two pieces. The map was together once again.

## A New World

THE WORLD looks different after you've narrowly avoided joining the Hawaiian Army. Colors seem brighter. Every breath seems like a gift, and every cigarette a treasure.

There was a spring in my step, so much so that people told me to stop doing it.

My mind was expanding. Or maybe my brain was expanding. Something was expanding.

The sunshine seemed warmer, the breeze cooler, and my pants seemed to fit better.

I felt generosity toward all mankind. I gave my stapler to a leper.

I noticed things I had never noticed

before, like the dew on the spiderweb and the blood on the giant spiderweb.

I was aware, for the first time, of all the meth pipes in the weeds and all the used condoms on the sidewalk.

The town stench seemed more complex than I remembered, and the ravings of the street lunatics much more subtle.

"Feeling better?" said Don. I put up my hand for him to hold that thought, as I was busy noticing things.

## *You?!*

By the time we got back to the hotel I wasn't noticing things so much, which was a relief. I borrowed fifty paleekas from Don and set off down the street.

I had just turned a corner when I saw a dreadful sight. It was Uncle Lou, with his dog, Screwball! My sore tooth began to throb. I ducked down behind a pickle barrel, and peeked out. A thug stopped Uncle Lou, brandishing a knife. Uncle Lou knocked him out with one punch. A pimp approached him with a young girl. Uncle Lou knocked him out and the girl ran off. A juggler approached and was quickly knocked out.

What was Uncle Lou doing here? Did he finally get that Tomlin transplant he was always talking about? I had a bad feeling about this.

He pulled out some little electronic gizmo, looked at it, and started toward me. I was trapped. I looked around for a place to hide. I decided to climb inside the pickle barrel. But I would need something to breathe through. Anything! I spotted a snorkel tube and diving mask lying nearby. I started to put on the flippers, too, but there was no time. I lowered myself into the brine. Somehow I was able to breathe through the snorkel. "He's around here somewhere," I heard Uncle Lou say. I looked up to see him through the floating pickles. He picked one up and bit into it. Screwball was scratching on the side of the barrel. "Come on, let's go," he said, jerking the dog away. I heard his big boots tromp off.

I fell asleep. There's something about breathing through a snorkel, suspended in pickle brine, that really makes you sleepy. I woke up when the shop owner tipped me over and poured me out.

I didn't tell Don about seeing Uncle Lou. He'd get upset. Don's tender. But I told him we should head upriver right away, and he agreed. We would leave early the next day. Seeing Uncle Lou had been a wake-up call.

# A Rocky Start

I OVERSLEPT the next morning. I crammed some clothes and packs of cigarettes around the scotch bottles to prevent breakage, and started waddling as fast as I could to the wharf. Don was on the boat, motioning for me to come on, then motioning at his watch. Don's always motioning about something.

As I climbed aboard, Don seemed surprised by my case of scotch. People are always surprised when you plan ahead.

We weighed anchor, cast off, and did some other nautical things. I want to say "screwed the pony," but that's not right.

Bizzy was standing on the bank, watching

us go by. I waved, but he didn't wave back. I guess waving is an American thing. For a second it looked like he was going to wave, but he was just scratching his whiskers. Then he spit to the side. That's sort of a wave, isn't it? I wondered what Bizzy was like as a child. I bet he was cute.

Don introduced me to the crew. First, there was Frenchy, the wily old veteran. He knew the river like the back of his hand.

Then there was Peleke. He was young, brash, and cocky. But if you were in a tough situation, he's who you wanted by your side.

Pip was always making us laugh. But there seemed to be something a little sad about him.

Next there were the twins, Greg and Greg Jr. Or maybe they were father and son, I'm not sure. But you could count on them to keep the engine running smoothly.

Finally, there was Chicken Skin. I don't remember much about him.

*      *      *

We headed upriver, into the vast, untamed vastness of Hawaii. Gradually, the smell of Honolulu faded and was replaced by the smell of the crew. At last, we were on our way.

We hadn't gone far when something happened that I took as an ill omen: we were attacked by a huge swarm of bats.

The bats flapped about our heads, scratching and biting us without mercy. They were like a tornado, only not a regular tornado—a tornado of bats. We tried to slap them away, but they were relentless. What were bats doing out in the daytime? That's when I noticed the solar eclipse, which didn't seem like a good sign, either.

When the sun finally came back, the bats went away, but then we were attacked by pelicans. Their beaks jabbed and poked us as we scurried for cover. I jumped over the side, but even underwater the pelicans dove on me. I was like a defenseless little baitfish.

I pulled myself onto the riverbank and ran into the jungle. I collapsed on the ground. I looked up to see spiders! Hundreds of them! I ran back to the water and jumped in.

The boat pulled alongside. "Are you okay?" said Don. Oh, great. Now *questions*.

The crew all quit right there. We had only gone about a hundred yards, so they just walked back to town along the bank. Then they started running, because of the mosquitoes. I think Pip said something funny as he ran, but I couldn't quite hear him.

We dropped anchor. Don and I just sat there for a while. "Maybe we should give up," Don sighed.

I shook my head and laughed. He asked me what I was thinking. I told him I was thinking about the episode of the *Two Stupid Idiots* where they're mistaken for astronauts. They fly their rocket through a barn, then into a tunnel so a train has to back up at superfast speed. Finally they crash into a mansion, where they blow up the evil villain, and then they get medals.

Don pursed his lips and nodded. "I see what you're saying. They could have given up, but they didn't."

Where'd he get *that*?

# Up the Paloonga

WE RESUMED our journey up the mighty Paloonga River. In the distance a delicate wisp of smoke rose from Mount Palinka. It was a picture worth a million paleekas.

There's a strange allure to this land. You can see why Robinson Crusoe was so attracted to it and stayed here for so long. For one thing, food grows right on the trees. You have to pick it, that's the only catch.

In the jungle you come to realize that death is a part of life. The bat eats the moth. Then the giant moth sucks the life out of the bat. Then the monkey eats the giant moth, pulling the wings off first, because he doesn't like that part. Then the monkey gets a parasite from the moth that slowly eats his brain. It's all part of the beautiful circle of life.

The jungle—and I'm not going to lie to you about this—is hot. Think of the hottest, most humid day you've ever had. Okay, not that hot, but almost that hot, that's my point.

I noticed the trail of a jet airliner far overhead. It seemed so odd that we would be cramped up in this stifling heat, with little monkeys screaming all around, while up there people were stretched out in quiet, air-conditioned luxury.

As we motored upriver, we saw some native men on the shore. "Look, they're waving to us," I said.

"Those men aren't waving," said Don. "They're pounding their roots. They've gathered roots, and now they're pounding them."

Man, doesn't anybody wave around here?

We came to a bunch of buildings on an island. It was the Hawaii Home for

Murderers. Hawaiians believe that murderers should be isolated from the rest of society. It sounds cruel and harsh to us, but that's the way they think. The inmates were all dressed in identical uniforms of bright flowery design.

From the brochure I learned that most murderers are not the crazy mass murderers you hear about. In fact, most murderers have only murdered one or two people. And most of those were either relatives or someone who gave them a bad look.

We sailed past the main yard, where hundreds of murderers were square dancing. I found out later it was actually a riot.

As we went by, a few of them waved at us. *Finally*, someone waves!

# *Memories*

I DON'T know why Don bothered to hire a crew in the first place. He was doing everything: driving the boat, checking the map, fixing the meals, cleaning up. He asked me to help clean up, but I don't know how to do that.

We pulled into shore for the night. Don built a fire, and I shared some of my scotch with him. I also applied some soothing scotch to my bat bites, pelican bites, and spider bites. And to some other weird thing I had.

I started reminiscing about the great friends we'd made on this trip. Frenchy, and Peleke, and of course little Pip. I'd probably miss him the most.

I thought about my girlfriend back in America. What was her name again? It was something like "Snargaret."

Just as I was missing her, Don told me a story that made me even sadder. It was about a priest and a rabbi going into a bar with a gorilla, and the priest ordering something but the bartender asking the gorilla for his ID, something like that. I forget the rest, but it was really sad.

To cheer us up, I decided to tell a joke. You need jokes to keep your morale up. And I told the dirtiest joke I could think of, to also keep our sexuality up.

Don went to bed. As the shadows from the fire danced on the trees, I did my funny cowboy dance and hit my head on a tree.

## The Pelican God

I WOKE up screaming, "There are spiders all over my face!" like I do every morning. But this time there really were spiders all over my face. Don rushed over and helped me brush them off.

"It's a good thing it's not spider season," he said. *Not spider season?!*

Don went off to the boat, to do whatever he does there. As I gazed up I saw something odd. It looked like a sheet of white paper, floating in the air. But as it circled down to me I realized, That's no piece of paper, that's a pelican!

If you've learned anything by now, it's that it's useless to run from a pelican. So instead, I closed my eyes tight and dropped to my knees. I prayed to the Pelican God and said that I would renounce all other gods before him.

When I opened my eyes, the pelican was gone. It was a miracle.

When Don came back, I asked him if he would convert to Pelicanism, but he said no.

Don was really starting to annoy me. He never called me Wrong Way Slurps or any of my other nicknames. Plus he was always ordering me around. "Would you please help me with this?" he would say, or "If you're not too busy, maybe you could give me a hand over here." Things like that. He kept pecking at my head, like a woodpecker. He started asking me stupid questions, like why had I brought scotch but not a hat.

"Well, you didn't even bring a *brain*," I said. Whenever anybody says an insult to you, just repeat it back to him by putting *brain* in there somewhere. Here's another example: Say someone says something like

"Do you have any idea where you are?" Just say, "Do you have any idea where your brain is?" Try it—it works with everything.

"Besides, I did bring a hat," I said. I put a pair of my underpants on my head and told him it was a beret.

# The Institute

I TOSSED some beef jerky to the alligators that were following the boat. Don complained about that, too.

Just to make him mad, I started eating candy bars and potato chips and throwing the wrappers overboard. Also cigarette butts. Personally, I didn't see the harm. There was no litter anyplace in the jungle, so what difference was it going to make?

"Hey, Don," I said, "is that a rare tropical frog?" I said, pointing to a Snickers wrapper as it floated away.

I thought about channeling my anger, but it was still kind of early. So instead I started coming up with ideas for inventions.

That's when I came up with the idea for the voodoo doll with interchangeable heads, so you don't have to get a new doll every time you want to put a curse on somebody. The basic head would be the Don head.

I littered for miles. I was starting to get bored when, out of the blue, a patch of bright green appeared. I was tickled pink. It was a golf course, with a big clubhouse set in the middle. Finally, something in Hawaii that was *pretty*.

"This isn't a golf course," said Don. "This is the Ponzari Institute."

"*Huh?*"

"It was founded by Doctor Ponzari, a famous scientist and philanthropist. He cured the plague in Honolulu. He's even won the Nobel Prize. I wrote to him from America, and he's invited us to stay with him on our way upriver."

"*Huh?*"

Two servants met us at the dock and carried our stuff, which was nice because my arms were tired from littering. We passed several other guests who were reading, strolling, and engaging in lively conversation. It was like a bad dream.

I asked a couple of girls if they wanted to come see my little hula statue. They said no.

# The Grounds

THIS DOCTOR Ponzari, whoever he was, was doing all right for himself.

The main house was a grand two-story made out of pineapple wood, the most precious of Hawaiian woods. Inside the great hall was a priceless set of antique wooden surfboards. Overhead was a collection of Viking battle-axes, hanging from the rafters by their wooden handles. Also on display was the very first US space capsule, which, I never knew, was made out of wood.

Outside, wooden walkways connected everything. On the lawn there was a giant upright hammer, stuck in the ground by its wooden shaft. Apparently it was some kind of artwork. People were meditating on the grass right below it.

There was even a wooden roller coaster to provide amusement for the guests.

The whole place was powered by a generator that ran on gas from human feces. The feces were stored in a huge wooden tank that sat up on wooden stilts, right next to the swimming pool.

Stacks of wooden beehives supplied fresh honey. "Those bees are harmless now," said the guy, "but if anything ever happened to those wooden boxes, Katy bar the door." I laughed. I know someone named Katy.

A teakwood observation deck extended out over a pool of piranhas.

There were even wooden cages holding wild animals that Doctor Ponzari had hand-raised after their mothers had rejected them.

I think my favorite thing was the old cannon. It was actually loaded, but they said the only way it could go off was if the wooden wheels suddenly collapsed and it fell hard. It was aimed at the house.

# *Breakfast at Ponzari's*

DOCTOR PONZARI was seated at a table in his flower garden. As soon as I saw him I could tell that he was pure evil. I've only had that feeling a few times in my life. I'd say about forty or forty-five times. My mailman is pure evil.

He was wearing a crisp linen suit. I wondered how many hundreds of people had died making it. His movements were elegant and refined, like some evil shitbird from Hell. He was eating a banana, elegantly.

He rose to greet Don and me. "Ah, there you are," he said, probably lying. "It's always nice to see fellow Americans. Please make yourselves at home and stay as long as you like."

When he shook my hand he tried to look me in the eye, but I knew better than that. "Very nice to meet you, Mister Slurps," he said. How did he know my name? Maybe he could read my mind. Or maybe he could read the questionnaire I had filled out. "I apologize for not greeting you at the dock. I was giving a lecture."

Oh, a "lecture." I guess that was his word for insane rant.

Don made the mistake of asking what his lecture was about. Never ask someone that. Doctor Ponzari said it was about his efforts to breed a new coconut that was meatier, insect-resistant, and drought-tolerant. In other words, a monster coconut.

Breakfast appeared magically on the table before us. I started to ask if I could get it "to go," but Doctor Ponzari proceeded to offer some advice. He urged us to give up our quest for the Golden

Monkey. "Not worth it, too dangerous to go upriver."

Don and I looked at each other. "What makes you think we're seeking the Golden Monkey?" said Don.

"Everyone does," said Ponzari. He added: "My brother-in-law has seen the Golden Monkey."

"Who's your brother-in-law, the Queen of Sheba?" I muttered.

"Actually, he's a department head at Cornell University."

Which one is that, I thought, the Department of Sheba?

Just to show off, Ponzari started telling us the history of the Golden Monkey. As soon as I heard the word *history* I stopped listening. I started listening again when I heard the words *missionary position*.

"The missionary position was that natives should not worship the Golden Monkey," said Ponzari.

A little blond-haired boy interrupted,

carrying two baseball gloves and a ball. "Father, you promised you'd play catch."

"Gentlemen, if you'll please excuse me, duty calls."

Doctor Ponzari was clearly evil, but when I saw him playing catch with his son, I thought, What a spaz.

# *Theories*

I HAVE to admit, after a while I came to enjoy Doctor Ponzari's place. I guess that's the nature of evil. I enjoyed doing cannonballs off the wooden diving board with all the sunbathers watching. I enjoyed teasing the animals in their cages, especially the lion and the gorilla. And I loved ringing the big cast-iron bell. "Hey, everyone, it's midnight!"

Don and Doctor Ponzari discussed the causes of child derangement. I already know the cause: sugar. And not enough spankings.

Most of Ponzari's guests were members of a group that has preyed on the fears of mankind for centuries: scientists. They had been invited by Doctor Ponzari to discuss world problems. Here's an idea: discuss the solutions instead.

Hanging around scientists makes you come up with scientific theories yourself. You can't help it; they just pop out. Here are some I came up with while I was there:

Birds evolved from dinosaurs, but guess what dinosaurs evolved from. That's right, birds.

A skeleton is more afraid of you than you are of him.

The more you flip something, like a pancake, the more flippable it becomes.

If Superman ever visited Tarzan, at first they'd get along, but then Superman would finally have to say, "How can you live like this?"

Street signs would work better if they added the words *You Idiot*. For instance, instead of just Stop, the sign says Stop, You Idiot.

When you howl to make your dog howl, he's not howling to sing along, he's telling you to shut up.

If you put your shoes on the wrong feet and walk around, eventually you will split in half.

The best thing about going to outer space is being able to go to a party and say, "I've been to outer space—where've you been?"

When you die you become pure energy, but it's not what we call a "usable" kind of energy.

Humans are evolving into a higher form and a lower form at the same time. Confused? Then guess which one you are.

# Escape

I PRETENDED to be perfectly relaxed and even interested in what Doctor Ponzari was saying. Then I threw my drink in his face. He screamed in pain as I ran to the door. It was locked. Desperately I fumbled at the latch, until finally I got it open. "This is the stupidest party I've ever been to!" I shouted as I ran out into the night.

Soon I was back in my jail cell. That's what I called my guest room. It was so nice and luxurious you didn't want to leave. It was like you were a prisoner.

Doctor Ponzari sent over a bottle of champagne and some fancy appetizers, along with a note saying he hoped he hadn't said anything to offend me. Don said I should go apologize to Doctor Ponzari, but I said Don should apologize to me for bringing us there in the first place. And for being Don.

I turned on the light only long enough to read Doctor Ponzari's apology, then quickly turned it off. I don't really like reading or doing much else by feces light.

As I sat there in the dark on my king-sized pillow-top bed, drinking the champagne and wondering how I could get hold of some more of those fancy appetizers, I had a weird thought: had I been rude to throw my flaming brandy into Doctor Ponzari's face, just because the going-away party he had thrown for us was so boring?

To snap myself out of it, I decided to go exploring. I put on my velvet guest robe and grabbed a flashlight. *Ahh, battery light.*

The great hall was still and quiet. I accidentally knocked over the fireplace tools, then straightened them, then somehow knocked them over again. I carefully reset them before moving on.

I came to Doctor Ponzari's laboratory. I started to jimmy the lock on the door, but it was already open. Don't you feel stupid when that happens? I went inside.

Lying loose on the window seats were brackets and matching curtain rods. I assumed the clamps were used to suspend people while experiments were done on them. I shudder to think what the curtain rods were for.

There was a tall wooden bookshelf, lined with rows of coconuts. Right below it was Doctor Ponzari's chair.

Normally, when you go through someone's desk, you don't find much. Usually just papers that you have to toss over your shoulder. But in the back of the bottom drawer was something different. Inside a simple, satin-lined case was a beautiful gold medallion, complete with a ribbon so you could wear it around your neck. It had a picture of Abraham Lincoln on one side and, on the other, two topless lesbians fondling each other. I had never seen anything so exquisite. I had to have it!

So it wouldn't be stealing, I decided to leave something behind. But what did I own that was worth as much? Only one thing: my beautiful stenchite hula girl. Or maybe my longhorn belt buckle. No, the hula girl. How, you're asking, could I leave such a valuable gift? If there's one thing I've learned in this life, it's that you can't just take; you also have to give. Plus, I'd had several glasses of champagne.

I went and got my hula girl, knocking over the fireplace tools again. *Who designs those things?!*

I unwrapped the little statue and started to set her down on the corner of Ponzari's oaken desk. I hesitated. Something the souvenir shop owner had said rang in my ears: "That's the storeroom. That's not the restroom. I hope you didn't do anything in there." It's weird the things that pop into your head, isn't it?

I gave my hula girl one last tap. Doctor Ponzari needed to get a new desk, because, as she danced, little cracks started spreading out from her.

# A Strange Noise

THE NEXT morning Doctor Ponzari saw us off at the dock. There was an odd creaking and splitting noise coming from somewhere. He noticed it, too. I guess the house was settling.

Ponzari tried to get us to stay longer. He said they were going to take the wild animals into the jungle the next day and release them. Oh, yeah, that would be interesting. He also offered to give us jobs if we wanted. Why is it that only evil people can offer you a job?

As we turned upriver, he gave us what I thought was a fakey, insincere wave. I waved back. Why am I so nice? I guess because of the way I was brought up; if someone does something to you, you do it back.

I missed my hula girl, I have to admit. But I felt that by graduating from hula girl to shiny medallion, I had grown as a man. The medallion reflected a bright beam of sunlight, which I aimed into Don's eyes. "What's that?" he said, blocking the light with his hand.

"Doctor Ponzari gave it to me," I replied.

It must have been a good lie, because Don seemed to believe it. "He's a generous man," he said. Don, maybe you and Doctor Ponzari should go get married and live forever on Ponzari Island.

We had only gone a few miles when we heard the strangest racket. It started as a long, loud, cracking noise, similar to the one we'd heard earlier, then turned into a tremendous rolling crash, going on and on, almost like a whole house falling down. Mixed in there were shrieks, what sounded like bee buzzing and vicious animal roars, more shrieks, a cannon firing, and a squishy hammer sound. Finally, in a wave, came the choking stink of feces.

At first we thought maybe the commotion came from Doctor Ponzari's, and we started to turn around. But then I noticed the flock of parakeets nearby. They were flapping and pooping and screeching away, making all sorts of crazy noises. One even sounded like coconuts rolling off wooden shelves and bouncing off someone's head. Nature is amazing.

Don wasn't entirely convinced it was the parakeets, but we continued upriver anyway.

# The Point of No Return

WE SAILED on and on, into the unknown. How strange that we have explored the moon and the other planets and yet we know so little about Hawaii.

"Have you noticed someone is following us?" Don said. I started to say, "Have you noticed your brain is following us?" but I realized he was serious.

I tried to take a look through the binoculars, but Don told me to wait until we got the strap off from around his neck, which took us a few minutes. By then the boat had dropped below the bend.

I had a bad feeling about this. Following does not usually end well. One time I started following this actress. It's not like I'm crazy; I was just obsessed with her. I asked Don the same question I asked the judge: "Just because something is behind something, is it actually 'following'?" Don had the same answer as the judge. "Yes, it's following."

We came to a sign floating on a buoy. The words on the sign would give a chill to any sane man: Entering National Park.

A ranger came out from a rustic, unpainted hut at the end of a ramshackle pier. Admission to the park was five paleekas. *"Five paleekas?!"* I said, as Don paid it. The ranger gave us brochures. Hawaiians love brochures. We had to hang a pass on the boat.

Suddenly the ranger's face began twitching. His features twisted and contorted into a horrible, snarling demon. His eyes flared. It was the scariest thing I'd ever seen. His voice became deep and echoey. He pointed at us as he issued this warning: As long as we stayed in the park, the pass was good. But if we left the park, and came back in, we would have to pay another admission fee.

He relaxed his face back to his regular look. I wish I could do that scary face. It really gets your point across.

I handed the ranger his bifocals, which had fallen off. He said thanks. We motored upriver.

The brochures were the usual stuff about lost civilizations, man-eating plants, and towering waterfalls. As I tossed them overboard, one caught my eye. It was about a weird half-man, half-turtle creature. Turtle men. They were said to be the souls of ancient warriors.

The brochure said not to feed them.

# The Ruins

THE JUNGLE grew darker and more mysterious. Bugs seemed buggier, and the trees
almost seemed alive. The sun was like a
blazing ball of fire in the sky. Strange little
birds hovered over flowers, stabbing them
with their long, pointed beaks. Sinister rock
formations appeared on shore and even
reached up out of the water. I guess that's
where Hawaii got its famous nickname,
"Land of a Thousand Nightmares."

Dark clouds gathered overhead. Then,
without warning, it began to rain. And it
kept raining, on and on. Who would have
thought it would rain so much in the jungle?

It must have rained for nearly twenty

minutes. Not hard the whole time, but still, raining. Don said to get used to it, because it was going to rain a lot more than that.

Oh, great, now Don's a weatherman.

When the mist cleared, something amazing began rising up from the jungle. Then I realized, it wasn't rising up; we were getting closer. It was the fabulous ruins of an ancient civilization.

As a joke, I pretended to be asleep. Don kept trying to wake me up, but I would not wake up. Good joke, huh? Then I pretended to wake up, see the ruins, and go right back to sleep.

I have to admit, the ruins were impressive. But like so many civilizations, they forgot the one rule that might have saved them: don't let vines grow all over you.

We stopped and looked around. There was a huge stone obelisk. I fell down and worshipped it. Then I felt bad that I had betrayed my Pelican faith. I asked Don if he would help me desecrate the obelisk, but he ignored me.

We moved on to a big outdoor stadium, where vicious ball games were played, and where spectators ate roasted dogs.

Nearby was a ceremonial hall. Men would gather there to chant and drink fermented beverages, in hopes of transporting themselves to another realm.

Towering above everything was the Great Temple. That was where the sacrifices were held. Like most advanced cultures, they had made the huge leap to killing people. Probably they started out squashing bugs, and they noticed that as a result, things got a little better. Then they sacrificed bigger animals, and things really improved. The breakthrough came when some genius pointed to another guy and said, "Let's kill *him*."

# An Ancient Clue

DON WAS motioning to me again. Just to annoy him I kept pointing to myself and mouthing, *Me?*

He had found an entrance to the Great Temple. Guarding the doorway was a statue of a man with a big cactus thorn through his penis. I think it meant "No Refunds."

We stepped inside. As my eyes adjusted to the dark, I beheld a wondrous sight. Fantastic painted murals covered the walls. I was floored. They depicted every kind of sex act you could imagine, and some you could never think of in a million years. They were the dirtiest pictures I had ever seen. Truly, these people were way advanced.

But Don was interested in something else. He called me over to a series of carvings that told a story. They showed a man swimming a river, climbing a mountain, and arriving at what looked like the Golden Monkey. Then going back and telling the others not to go. What did it mean?

# Ride the Wild Wind

THAT NIGHT, around the campfire, Don asked me what I was going to do with my share of the treasure.

"You'll think it's silly," I said.

He promised he wouldn't, so I told him. "I've always wanted a big top hat with a little cannon that would come out, fire, then go back in the hat."

He looked at me for a moment, and nodded.

I asked him what he was going to do with his share. He said he was thinking about buying a starter home and seeing if his ex-wife would maybe give it another try. It was hard to keep from laughing. Yeah, good plan.

As the campfire dwindled, and Don dwindled off to sleep, I got an idea. At first I was worried it wasn't a good idea, but I'd had two scotches, and every idea I've ever had after two scotches has been a good one.

It's not easy climbing up ancient, vine-covered steps, at night, with a glass of scotch in one hand and a cigarette in the other. A big block of stone broke loose and tumbled down the steps toward me. I jumped out of the way just in time. I checked my scotch. Whew! Finally, I made it to the slippery, narrow platform at the top.

I spun around and around, holding my arms up in wonder to the immense, starry sky. The wind rushed through my hair. For a moment I thought I might achieve man's age-old dream of hair-powered flight.

These ruins were surely the most amazing place on Earth.

# *Mementos*

BY MORNING, I'd had enough of the ruins. If you're like me, a little ancient ruin goes a long way. It makes you want to go back in a time machine and tell them, "Quit building these things!" All I wanted was a souvenir and to get going.

The trouble with ancient things is they don't break off cleanly, even with a sledge-hammer. Most of the time they shatter. And if you do manage to get one off whole, the color fades away when you take it out into the sunlight. I finally gave up.

Don wanted to get some photos. I decided to make the photos funny. In the one where I'm sitting by a big statue of a mongoose, I act like the mongoose is biting my arm. In the one with the lizard statue, I put a lit cigarette between its lips. "Look, the lizard's smoking!" I seem to be saying. It didn't make any sense!

There was a giant stone statue of a warrior, striding forward. I put a banana peel under his front foot. Just as I was pointing at the banana peel and laughing, and Don was about to take the picture, we heard a truck coming toward us through the jungle.

It turned out to be a jeep, not a truck. Jeep, truck, does it really make that much difference? Don and I hid behind the mongoose.

At first I didn't recognize him. He had a bandage covering the top of his head, and what looked like multiple gorilla bites across his face. And bee stings all over his hands and neck.

It was Doctor Ponzari.

His fancy suit had splinters sticking out all over. That's the trouble with linen.

He got out of the jeep with a groan. "Good afternoon, gentlemen," he called out. He held up my hula girl. "I believe this is yours, Mister Slurps. It has your initials on the bottom: W.W.S., for Wrong Way Slurps. This little trinket destroyed the entire Ponzari Institute. Fortunately, no one was killed."

"What's he talking about?" whispered Don.

"I don't know," I said, trying to figure out how to cup my hand around my mouth but finally giving up. "He's insane."

"Please come out, Mister Slurps. And if it's not too much trouble, I must ask you to talk to this gentleman here." Ponzari indicated a short man in a stripy suit with a briefcase. "He's with the insurance company."

Don said, "Maybe we should talk to them."

"I am prepared to wait here indefinitely," said Ponzari. He stuck his arm straight out and leaned nonchalantly against the gigantic stone warrior. He shouldn't have done that. The pressure was just enough to make the statue slip on the banana peel and crash down on top of them.

*"AAAAGGGHHHEE!"* shrieked Doctor Ponzari. The whole thing happened as if in slow motion. Ponzari tried to dive away but was doomed to be flattened. The insurance man never saw it coming. He was standing straight up as the colossus struck him. It sheared off one side of his skull, and his remaining eyeball shot out of its socket, followed by a torrent of blood and gray gunk. Both his shinbones broke in half and stuck out through his pants. His spine snapped loose and curled over his shoulder like a snake. Finally, his rib cage collapsed like an accordion, with some sort of liquid squirting out between the ribs.

The statue landed with a tremendous *thud*. Dust and leaves *whooshed* up. Birds and monkeys screamed.

Don and I just looked at each other. And ran, toward the boat.

"Wait!" said Don. "Let's try to lift it!"

I swear, we lifted and lifted on that statue, but it wouldn't budge. Except for the cheeping of some angry gophers, all was quiet.

# *Carrying On*

WHEN SOMETHING bad happens, there's a tendency to think that somehow you did something to cause it. That has happened to me many times. But it's just your brain. Ignore it. Look on the bright side: the evil reign of Doctor Ponzari was over. No longer would he inflict his "cures" and "discoveries" on people. Also, the evil reign of the insurance man was over.

We decided to keep going. Even though Doctor Ponzari was in Hell now, being tortured with hot branding irons, I felt that he would have wanted us to continue.

Don radioed Honolulu and told them what had happened, so the relatives could come and dig out the badly decomposed bodies.

As I sat there waiting on the fallen statue, a miracle occurred: I spotted my little hula girl! She was just lying there. When I picked her up and dusted her off, she did her little dance for me. I almost cried.

We headed upriver, not forgetting Doctor Ponzari, but not remembering him, either. "We have to stay focused on the Golden Monkey," I said before taking a nap.

I was awakened by the sounds of Don setting up "camp," whatever that is. I went off to explore. By the way, underpants make a perfectly good hat. Here's a tip: put the leg hole over your head, not the waist hole.


There is life everywhere in the jungle, if you take the time to look. Over there, on that open patch, there are ants. On that tree trunk, climbing up and down, is a column of ants. And floating on the pond are ants.

There are orchids all over the place.

You think you'd never get tired of seeing orchids, but there are so many it kind of makes you mad.

I came upon a beautiful wild parrot. I thought if I could catch him, I could train him to talk. I'd teach him to say, "Don is a big stupid jerk." I chased that parrot for the longest time. He would squawk and I would squawk back. Every time I squawked back he would drop a piece of breadfruit to me, as a reward. But I had to do the exact same squawk that he did. He was very patient, repeating the squawk over and over until I got it right.

If you've never tasted breadfruit, it tastes kind of like a cracker. Man, I want that breadfruit.

# *Leilani*

I WENT deeper into the jungle. That's when I first saw her. Leilani. She was the most beautiful thing I had ever seen, and I'm not just saying that because she was nude.

She was showering beneath a crystal-clear waterfall. Sparkles of water glistened on her breasts, and threw prisms of light onto the lenses of my binoculars.

She glanced over and saw me. She grabbed her basket and bounded off into the woods. She was like a deer, only a two-legged deer with a really nice ass. "Come back!" I yelled. "I only want to have sex with you!"

I went back to the boat and got a fishing

net. I don't like to catch a girl in a net just to meet her, but if I have to I will.

What is the one thing every woman loves? Pretty rocks, right? They like to pick them up and show them to you. I gathered some rocks from the stream bed that I thought would appeal to the woman brain. Then I laid them at the foot of a tree, with the net resting in the branches overhead.

I hid behind the tree and waited. I heard a squeal and set the net. But guess what I caught: a wild pig! I had to laugh. One minute beautiful girl, the next minute angry insane pig. What are the odds of that ever happening?

I gathered up the net and tried to fold it, but somehow it got wrapped all around me. I rolled down the hill. Every time I got up I toppled over and rolled farther down the hill. I cried out for help, in a fierce, manly way.

There was a knife at my throat. It was the girl. I recognized her face, but not the rest of her, because she was wearing clothes: the traditional grass skirt and coconut bra.

"Why you want catch Leilani?" she hissed.

I had to think fast. I made up a lie. "I was going to sell you to a carnival."

She spat in my face. I was in love.

Don came running up. Leilani turned to face him. "Put the knife away," said Don. They stared at each other for a moment. Then, for some reason, she did put the knife away. And ran off into the jungle. Don ran after her. "No one want hurt you," he yelled like a baby.

So, Don was already moving in on my girl. I should have known. For one thing, he likes native girls. His favorite movie is *Native Girl*, starring Marlene Dietrich.

Also, I think he wants to get back at me for dating his ex-wife, Debby. It's true, Don and Debby were going through couples therapy when I started dating her, but they were separated—that's the point I'm trying to make. Also, as I have said many times, she broke up with me, too, so who's the real victim here?

It took Don about an hour to get me out of the net. I was wrapped up tight, like a juicy ham.

That night, as I tried to massage the net marks out of my arms, legs, and face, I was thinking about one thing: Leilani. I was so much in love that even the pounding of the native drums didn't bother me. By about three in the morning the drums were bothering me, but I'd still say I was about 90 percent in love.

I was also thinking about my girlfriend back in America, and wondering if she would agree to dress up like Leilani.

# *Leilani Joins Up*

WHILE DON was finishing breakfast, I was busy naming ants. I hope if I ever get reincarnated I can make a deal where I come back as a million ants. That way, even if I get stepped on or attacked by an anteater, I don't care, because there's lots more of me where that came from.

I was running out of ant names—the obvious ones, anyway—when, from out of the morning mist, Leilani appeared. At first she just stood there, at the edge of the jungle, holding her basket. Was she real, or was she a vision? All of a sudden naming ants didn't seem so important.

She approached us confidently. The

sound of her flip-flops was like music. She sat down and dished herself some breakfast. No one said a word. Finally she turned to Don. "I guide you upriver. Fifty paleekas."

*"Fifty paleekas?! That's fine!"* I said.

The price went up to two hundred paleekas when she found out I was going, too. Was that good or bad? I still can't figure it out.

As Leilani and Don packed up the boat, I splashed on some aftershave, a musky fragrance called Midnight in Diarroa.

I tied Leilani's outrigger canoe to the back of our boat, and we set off upriver. Then we came back for the canoe and retied it.

Leilani knew every bend in the river. And soon, I hoped, I would know every bend on Leilani. I kept giving her come-on looks, but she gave me looks that could kill. In fact, two or three times she said, "Me kill you."

I tried to break the ice by asking her what the drums had been saying the night before. But she wouldn't answer. Maybe, Leilani, you should have paid more attention during drum class.

# *Mars*

THAT EVENING, I decided to make my move. Don was off gathering firewood or acorns or whatever it is he gathers.

I sat down on the log next to Leilani. She eyed me suspiciously. I used my standard opening line: "What's your religion?" She said she was a Christian. I said I worshipped the Pelican God. There was a long silence.

I hit her with my second-best line: "What's your favorite episode of the *Two Stupid Idiots*?" What I saw next was unbelievable. It was like looking into the face of a dog. She had absolutely no idea who the Two Stupid Idiots were. It was scary.

I showed her my medallion and told her I'd won it in a disco-dancing contest.

"You lie," she said. "That not yours."

Boy, things weren't starting off too well.

I pointed to a star in the sky. "There's Mars," I said. She shook her head and pointed to a different star. I continued: "Every time I see Mars, it makes me think of the first Martian to invent the flying saucer. The other Martians probably made fun of his invention. They called it the Blind Man's Flapjack and the Moron's Merry-Go-Round. They didn't think anything could replace their precious rocket ship. But when the king of Mars decided to invade Earth, he went with the flying saucer. And the rest is history."

I had her in the right mood. As the full moon was peeking up over the palm trees, I stole a peek at her moon and slipped my palm around her.

"No touch coconuts," she said, pulling out her knife. I was nowhere near her coconuts!

Don came stumbling out of the trees. Thanks, Don, just when I was getting somewhere.

# The Red Boat

I DECIDED to change tactics with Leilani. Let the honey come to the bee. Let the cheese ball come to the toothpick. Let the triangle come to the triangle clanger.

As we chugged upriver, I stared off into space, like I was thinking of something. Leilani seemed to notice. But the boat hit a rough patch of rapids. It's hard to pretend you're thinking deeply when you're bouncing up and down, trying to hold on to the railing, your head jerking back and forth.

Don kept looking behind us. "I'm afraid I've got some bad news," he said. Surprise,

surprise. "The boat that was following us is back."

There it was, bright red and belching smoke everywhere, just like Uncle Lou. It was gaining on us.

"They catch us," said Leilani. She pulled out her knife. Man, that's her answer for everything.

I got an idea. It's the same idea I've used a lot in my life. "Let's hide in the bushes." We could snuggle the boat into the bushes along the bank. Then wait until the red boat passed.

"Too dangerous go in bushes," said Leilani.

Don couldn't decide. When people can't decide, it's usually best to taunt them.

"What's the matter, Don?" I said. "Scared there might be some itty-bitty spiders in the bushes?"

"Let's outrun them," he said. He gunned the engine, but we started sputtering and slowed to a crawl, also like Uncle Lou.

"Countersink valve stuck!" said Leilani.

The pointy part of the red boat appeared around the bend. We had to do something, fast. Don backed us into the bushes and cut the engine.

I checked around for spiders.

# *Gloating*

W<small>E SQUATTED</small> down. No one made a sound, except for the accidental sound I made when I squatted.

The red boat approached. The man driving it looked vaguely familiar. I reached for the binoculars. How do these stupid focus deals work, anyway?!

The red boat chugged past us upriver. My plan had worked. I turned to Leilani. I wanted to gloat, but as a man I had other desires. I wanted to tell her how I had been right and she had been wrong. Wait, I guess that's gloating.

But before I could say anything, part of the bank across from us began to move.

It was another boat, covered with bushes. They must have gotten stuck, and now the bushes were stuck to their boat. I shook my head and snickered. I got to gloat after all.

It looked like a boatload of tourists to me. They were all badly dressed and covered with hideous scars.

"Ahoy!" yelled the captain, waving with both hands. Now *that's* a wave.

"Ahoy!" I yelled, waving back. "Are you lost?"

"Yes, we're lost. Do you have a map we could look at?"

The boat slowly came toward us.

"Not a regular map, just a treasure map," I said, hoping that would be okay. I got the feeling it was.

"Maybe the girl can help us," said the captain. "Maybe she can help all of us." He grinned at the others.

Don got out a flare gun. We have flare guns? Why didn't anyone tell me?

"Stay back!" Don shouted at the boat.

I tried to make conversation, to make up

for Don's rudeness. "Say, I like your vest. What's it made of?"

"Human skin," said the captain. They were tourists all right. One of them even had one of those hook-hands that tourists like to get.

"They're tourists," I said.

"They pirates," said Leilani.

# A Pirate's Laugh

THE BOAT inched closer. The captain started laughing. I guess he was thinking of a joke. Then he started gagging up blood. It must have been a really good joke.

I saw Leilani's knife sticking in his belly. The captain fell to the deck. The pirates let out a roar of murderous rage.

In a show of defiance, I wet my pants.

Don fired his flare gun. It skittered across the deck and caught the captain's beard on fire.

One pirate aimed a shotgun at us. An arrow came from out of nowhere and went through his neck. He staggered, then fired his shotgun into the back of the captain, who groaned. Another pirate brandished a pistol, but an arrow knocked it from his hand. A hatchet flew through the air right at us, only to be deflected by yet another arrow. The angry pirate made an obscene gesture at us. An arrow went through his middle finger. He screamed.

The captain rose up, his beard smoldering. He held a bundle of dynamite sticks. He lit the fuse with his beard, then leaned back to heave it at us. An arrow went through his head, like that comedian, what's-his-name.

The pirates all scrambled to pick up the dynamite, but it was too late. The boat blew apart.

Pirates and boat pieces were blasted sky-high. A few pirates were able to maintain their dignity in midair, but most were flipping and flailing out of control. After they hit the water, the alligators that had been following us made short work of them. It was a horrible sight. And after a while, to be honest, it got kind of monotonous.

Chomp-chomp-scream, chomp-chomp-scream. We get it.

A few pirates managed to crawl onto shore but were eaten by Komodo dragons.

The captain was carried off by a giant eagle. His dangling hand seemed to be waving.

One pirate almost made it into our boat. Don was even helping him aboard when an alligator reached up and pulled him back in. The alligator let the pirate climb out again before pulling him back in. He did that three times. I guess alligators have a sense of humor.

We heard the low, bubbly rumble of an engine. Through the smoke and still-falling shreds of pirate pants, something was moving toward us. That's when I saw a sight that made me wish I'd never been born, or that I'd been born as a fly. It was the red boat. And it was coming back.

At the wheel was a giant of a man, holding a loaded crossbow.

"It Bizzy!" said Leilani.

Bizzy, it turns out, had been following us all this time, to make sure we were okay. As a member of the Tourist Board, he was authorized to shoot and kill anyone bothering tourists. He made Don and me sign a paper saying we'd had a good time in Hawaii.

"Pirates bad for tourism," said Bizzy. "Give impression tourists come Hawaii, get robbed."

Bizzy could protect us no longer. He had to get back for a meeting of the Tourist Board. The board was divided over what type of tourist to attract. Bizzy did not favor the average tourist. They didn't spend enough money. Instead he favored the big-spending "prostitute tourist" like me. It was nice to know I was in the elite.

Bizzy asked Leilani how business was at Leilani's Leaves 'N Things. Leilani said things were slow now that the plague was back. *The plague was back?!*

"Say hi Bob Chapman for me," said Leilani.

"I do that," said Bizzy. He turned his boat downstream before tossing me a small box. Inside were my nose plugs. They fit perfectly.

Bizzy started to pull away. "Wait!" I yelled nasally. This was my chance to head back to Honolulu, and I wasn't going to miss it. I looked to Don and Leilani. They seemed to be saying, *Go back with Bizzy.* In fact, they did say that. They didn't want to endanger me any longer. But I couldn't do it. Leilani had specks of blood spattered across her face, like freckles. She was adorable. If I left, she would be totally bored by Don. No, I would have to stay. Besides, now that the pirates were dead, what danger could there be?

I turned to tell Bizzy to go on, but he had already left.

# *Radio Shack*

SEEING PEOPLE get eaten by alligators makes you think. Your first thought is, Boy, what a waste of pirates. Then you think, I'm glad that's not me. Then you think, I should take a video of this. Then you think, Damn, I left my camera at home. Then you think, Oh, yeah, it's broken anyway. Then you think, I wonder where I can get it fixed. Then you think, Radio Shack?

You can't help thinking about the families of the pirates. Every night a pirate's "old lady" would be patiently waiting for him at the back door. But never again would she hear the gentle tap of his peg leg on the porch, or hear him blaspheme when he saw the dog chewing on his spare peg.

She would gather her children round and try to explain, as gently as she could, that their father wouldn't be coming home, that he was stabbed in the belly, then he was shotgunned in the back, then an arrow went through his head, then he was blown up, then he was grabbed by an alligator and shaken back and forth like a rag doll before a giant eagle stole him from the alligator and carried him off to her nest, where he was pulled apart and fed to the eagle babies. Who excreted him.

She would go to the hutch and take down the pirate's favorite goblet, made out of a missionary's skull, and present it to her little boy. "I think he would want you to have this," she would say.

I did something I hadn't done in a long time: I broke down and cried like a baby. I hugged Don. He patted me on the back. I burped up some food on his shoulder.

# *Fishing*

DON AND Leilani didn't seem to share my emotional turmoil. They were more concerned with fixing the engine and moving cargo around so we could break free of the riverbank. I wish I could be that way.

I had to do something to get Leilani's attention. What does a woman love to see flopped down on the table in front of her? A fish, right? A fish that she could clean and season and cook and set before you, and hope more than anything that you liked.

I made a fishing pole out of an antenna thing from the boat. For fishing line, I used some wire connected to the antenna. For a hook, I used some gizmo from the radio.

Right away I hooked something big. It took me forever to pull it in. I finally got it to the surface so I could get a look at it. It was a dead pirate. A good-sized one, too. I released him. He drifted away, to fight another day.

# *Drums*

DON AND Leilani finally got the engine fixed. But when they started it up, I smelled smoke. "Get out, she's going to blow!" I yelled. We scrambled out of the boat and plunged headlong into the bushes. But the boat didn't blow up. We got up, dusted ourselves off, and cautiously approached the boat. That's when I got a weird feeling. "Get away!" I shouted. "She's going to blow again!" We flung ourselves behind rocks and trees. But she didn't blow that time, either. We were lucky.

Lured on by the Golden Monkey, and the chance that Leilani might take another outdoor shower, we sailed on. Deeper and deeper into the bowels of Hawaii. Would we ever come out of the bowels, and if so, would we be in one piece?

My mood brightened when a rainbow appeared over the river. What is it about a rainbow that enchants us and yet frightens us? If I knew that, I'd be a rich man. The rainbow turned into a double rainbow. Would it turn into a triple rainbow? I crossed my fingers. No, just a double rainbow. I hung my head in disappointment.

That night we heard drums. They were louder this time, which Don said was because we were closer and not because they were using bigger drums.

But couldn't it be that we were closer *and* they were using bigger drums? Don admitted it could.

Maybe we weren't any closer, but the drummers were hitting the drums harder. Don said that was unlikely.

Maybe our eardrums were getting better.

# Turtle Man

I WAS awakened by a blood-curdling scream-ing. At first I thought it was me, because I was having pelican nightmares. But it was Don, up in a tree, screaming his head off. I started to turn back to sleep.

That's when I spied the most horrible creature I'd ever seen (after Don's mother). It was standing right below Don, trying to stab him with a long, sharpened stick. It was roaring and snapping its slobbering jaws. It was a turtle man.

Leilani rushed forward with her knife. The turtle man knocked her backwards with one flip of its mighty flipper.

"Try to distract it!" yelled Don. I started

making out with Leilani, but she pushed me away. As I looked on helpfully, she picked up a frying pan, and sneaked up and banged the huge, vicious thing over the head. *Bong!* It stood there for a second, then fell dead.

"Leilani, you saved my life," said Don, alighting from the tree where he had clung like a frightened baboon.

"Yes, but at what cost?" I said, indicating the dead turtle man.

"I suppose we should report this to a park ranger," said Don. "Or bury him."

I had a better idea.


The great thing about turtle man is he cooks in his own shell. You basically use the shell as a big pot, pull him onto a fire, and he simmers in his own juices. Of course you have to pry off the breastplate and scoop out the guts, but that just takes a crowbar, a good knife, and a bucket. Then when the flippers and the head fall off, you put them in the shell with the rest of the meat. Like a stew.

"Umm, it's good," I said as I chewed on one of the handlike flippers. I think the flippers were the best part. I crunched down on something hard. It turned out to be a ring. It was pretty crude, so I threw it away.

Don and Leilani didn't want any turtle man. Leilani said it was taboo. I let it go. Once you start asking a woman what's taboo, you've got a long night ahead of you.

"Why would the turtle man attack us?" Don wondered.

I shrugged, in a way that said Don was stupid.

Just as I was cracking the turtle man's wishbone, and making a wish, I saw two pairs of eyes staring at me from inside a bush. I froze. Leilani noticed and stood up. Two little turtle men jumped out in a panic and ran off into the darkness.

"They babies," said Leilani.

They looked delicious.

# *Leftovers*

THE NEXT morning I was troubled. What were we going to do with all those leftovers? The problem with turtle man is there's so much of him. I could make a casserole, if I knew how to make a casserole. Or a sandwich, if I knew that.

As I wolfed down some cold turtle man, I tossed some scraps to the blue jays, who gobbled them. I gave Don a look that said, "So who's right, you or the blue jays? I'd say the blue jays."

As we headed upriver, Don got quiet. Whenever someone's quiet I like to ask him questions, to fill in the silence.

"Don, do you believe in God?"

"Yes, I do."

"Do you think the turtle man had a soul?"

"I'm not sure."

"If he had a soul, would he go to Heaven?"

"He probably would."

I burst out laughing. Turtle man in Heaven. It just made me laugh.

That's when it hit me: laughs. *Women love a man who makes them laugh!* And what's the one thing that makes women laugh? Puppets.

## Puppets and Pulp

LATER THAT day, as we sailed through a narrow stretch of river, I made a puppet out of a sock. It was actually just a sock, but if you make a funny high voice, it "becomes" a puppet.

"Hey, where's Leilani?" I said in the high voice. I made the sock turn from side to side, like he was looking around for something. Leilani pulled the puppet off my hand and threw it overboard.

What was *wrong* with her? Was she crazy? A pretty girl who was also crazy was something I'd never heard of.

I kept my cool. Calmly, slowly, I climbed

to the top of the cabin. I became perfectly still. Then, with a jolt, I began doing my funny cowboy dance. I pulled out all the stops. I did the "agitated leg while the other leg is straight," the tiptoe prance, the bow-legged forward scoot, and the galloping in place with eyes crossed.

The monkeys in the trees began screaming. Hold on monkeys, I'm just getting warmed up.

"Get down!" said Leilani. Oh, yeah, mama, I'm gettin' down. I did the cowboy peekaboo before switching to the pretending-to-lasso-something-that-pulls-you-off-your-feet.

"Get down!" Leilani yelled. She and Don hit the deck. Something stuck in my forehead. It was a blow dart. "Oww!" I moaned, because it hurt. Leilani pulled me down just as several more darts *ka-thunk*ed into the cabin.

I remembered the old Boy Scout saying: "Deal with the dart, That's where you start,

Then deal with the poison, And not vice-voison." I pulled the dart out and threw it away. But it stuck in my foot. I threw it away again.

My head started swimming. I began to shimmy uncontrollably, like Uncle Lou before the paramedics came. My whole body was heaving upward, like Uncle Lou when they applied the electric paddles to him. I began to curse hysterically, like Uncle Lou when he got the hospital bill.

Here's a tip: if your friend Don says, "Bite down on this," he means the stick in his hand, not his finger.

Leilani appeared, hovering over my face, chewing gum. No, wait, she's not chewing gum, she's chewing leaves. From her basket. She took the pulp out of her mouth and applied it to my forehead and my foot. As she leaned over me, I wanted to kiss her, but she had really bad leaf breath.

# Blow-Dart Dreams

IT FELT like elves were hammering nails into my head, but with no rhyme or reason.

Then it felt like I was rolling around on a bed of thumbtacks. But this was no party game.

Terrifying visions swirled through my head: an alarm clock going off; a riding lawn mower with my name on it; a man happily rocking from side to side, playing a banjo. The blow-dart poison was destroying my mind, and not in a good way.

I saw myself as a termite, feeling so proud of the tunnel I had dug with my own mouth.

I was on a crashing airplane. The old man next to me was praying. Down and down we went. I started hitting the old man with a rolled-up magazine, yelling, "Pray harder, old man!"

I imagined myself falling through the air, without a parachute. I landed on a big haystack. Then I fell off the haystack onto a bale of cotton. Then I fell onto the ground and really twisted my ankle.

I saw myself with a beehive stuck on my head. Then I saw myself putting a sombrero on top of it, so I could go to a costume party as a Mexican beehive.

I became a snowflake, drifting slowly to earth. I was different from every other snowflake, and they let me know it.

I was walking on a tightrope, high above the crowd. Suddenly the Human Cannonball went flying by, almost knocking me off. And I thought, What has become of circus safety standards?

I dreamed I was swimming upstream, fighting my way up waterfalls, until I came to a slow, shallow pool, where I laid my eggs.

I saw myself being dragged behind a horse by a bunch of rowdy cowboys. I wondered why they were dragging me, then I realized: it was my clean clothes and cheerful attitude.

I became a mummy, driving a car. And I thought, Why am I driving a car? Then I understood: I was plowing down pedestrians.

I was an angel in Heaven, eating a piece of pie. Another angel asked me where I got the pie. I just laughed and said, "Wouldn't you like to know."

I held a point of brilliant white light in my hands. It didn't even burn. Wait, now it's really starting to burn.

I saw the Pelican God, sitting on a throne. I threw him a fish, but he just looked at it. Then he began jabbing me with his heavenly beak.

I woke up. Leilani was poking me with a stick. "He okay now," I heard her say.

# Hangover

I DON'T know if you've ever had a blow-dart hangover, but they are the worst. It makes you swear never to get hit by one again.

I decided to make one last play for Leilani. If there's ever a time women will feel sorry for you, it's after you've been hit by a blow dart. But there would be no mercy this time. I would go for the "Nice Guy Approach." This is where you bring things to the woman and act like you're interested in what she's thinking. It's the dirtiest trick of all, and I usually don't like to use it.

Leilani was wiping motor grease off her

hands. It made her even sexier. I poured a couple of scotches, fluffed up my beret, and sat down next to her.

"I want to thank you for what you did," I said, pointing to my foot, which was three times its normal size. She didn't say anything. I continued: "But I don't understand. Who would want to shoot us with poison darts? Teenagers?"

*"Teenagers?"* said Leilani, irritated. "Not teenagers. Natives."

"Natives? But why?"

"White man steal land, bring disease, make native feel like stranger in own country."

I wanted to tell her, first of all, that Don and I were there to steal gold, not land. And second, what were the other things again?

Leilani set her scotch aside and started to get up. I stopped her. "Wait," I said, trying to look shy. "Maybe I shouldn't tell you this, but when I was unconscious, I dreamed I was kissing you. Your lips were warm and tender, and so were mine."

I closed my eyes, extended my tongue, and leaned over to kiss her. I tumbled overboard.

# *More Darts*

OVER THE next few days I was hit by at least twenty more blow darts. I was hit by several as I was standing on the front tip of the boat, pretending to be a hood ornament (as a joke). When I woke up, I asked Leilani how many blow darts had hit me. She seemed annoyed: "What, me your personal blow-dart counter?"

She wouldn't even chew up the mulch. She just left her basket of leaves next to me. You know things are going downhill when your girlfriend won't chew your mulch anymore.

Once I chewed the wrong leaf. It gave me a massive swelling of the pakeeni. I kept a few of those leaves.

More darts hit me. I think it was Gerald Ford who said that a man can only take so many blow darts before he snaps.

But then, after a while, the darts didn't bother me so much. I would get a headache and some cotton mouth, that was about it. I learned to swat most of them away like mosquitoes.

The most annoying thing was, why was I the only one getting hit? Even after I pinned a "Shoot Me" sign on the back of Don's shirt. Leilani claimed I was "paloonka," which means having a disruptive spirit that offends the very plane of the universe, upsetting the natural flow of events. How do you fight crazy native superstition like that?

# The Helicopter

WHILE DON and Leilani worked on the engine together, I went off to look for arrowheads. I collect arrowheads, if I ever find one.

I went farther and farther into the jungle. Arrowhead? No. Arrowhead? No. Arrowhead? No. Sometimes you wonder if the Pelican God even *cares* if you find an arrowhead.

Suddenly there was a weird popping sound. The palm trees began flapping around like Grandpa when the horseflies got him. A helicopter was hovering right above me.

I have never heard anything good coming from a bullhorn. And this was no exception. "Good afternoon, Mister Slurps."

It was Doctor Ponzari!

He was wearing a neck brace, and his leg was in a cast. The cast looked like it had been autographed by several people. His suit was dusty and torn, and his hands and arms were covered with gopher bites.

"Mister Slurps, I spoke with the insurance company, and they will not require you to talk to the claims adjustor. Besides, he's still in rehab," he said. "The insurance people say you just need to sign this form." He held up a clipboard. "And then I can submit a claim."

I did what I always do whenever someone wants me to sign a clipboard: I ran. The helicopter chased me through the jungle like the horseflies chased Grandpa. I stumbled and fell.

The helicopter was right above me and coming lower. I noticed the reflection from my medallion bouncing around in the shadows. I blew my breath onto the medallion and polished it with my beret. I aimed the beam into the eyes of the pilot.

*"AAAEEEEEE!"* he shrieked, clawing at his face.

The helicopter began spinning about wildly, drifting this way and that. Doctor Ponzari grabbed the stick to control it, but it was no use. The helicopter slammed into a sheer rock face and exploded. Then, as if trying to cling on to the cliff, the helicopter skidded down it and exploded again. Then sank into a swamp. There was silence, followed by a muffled explosion.

I thought about the pilot's wife. Each night when he came home, she would be waiting for him at the door with a rolling pin. He had a bad marriage.

# *Lost*

YES, DOCTOR **Ponzari was dead, but it had come at a horrible price: I was lost. In a split second, the jungle changed. No longer was it the friendly, happy place you normally think of. The scorpion wasn't the cute little spiky guy anymore, and the leeches all over your legs didn't seem quite so funny.**

**I staggered through the woods. I told myself to quit staggering, to stand up and walk straight. That would work for a while, but it's funny how strong that stagger instinct is.**

**There were times when I thought, I can't take another step. And there were times**

when I could barely crawl. And then there were times when I thought I could crawl forever.

I fell into some quicksand. I sank up to my waist. I flopped back and forth. Using all my strength, I was able to pull myself out. Later I found out that what I had fallen into is known as "fool's quicksand."

My bad luck continued. I tripped a native booby trap, and a sharp, wooden stake whipped around and hit me in the medallion, leaving a dent in it.

I looked around for some bugs to eat. If you get hungry enough, believe me, you will eat bugs. My friend Jerry found that out the hard way. He was slow getting the snacks out for a party once and we ate his butterfly collection.

I learned where to find water, and that you shouldn't look into a geyser hole when it's gurgling.

I built myself a nest of branches in a tree to sleep in. Soon I learned to tie the branches down so that when I lay down on them I wouldn't fall through.

I threw my clothes off. I found a tar pit and smeared my body with tar. Then I covered myself with feathers.

Crazy thoughts went through my head. Why, I wondered, would anyone invite the Two Stupid Idiots to launch a ship? And why would nitroglycerin come in a bottle that looked like a champagne bottle?

I ate fruit from the trees without even washing it.

I became aware of each moment.

I had become a brute savage.

# The Laughter of Children

I PONDERED my next course of action. Finally, I settled on a plan, and put it into motion. I had just begun my nap when I was awakened by the sound of children playing. Children playing? That could only mean one thing: I had to go tell them to be quiet.

I followed the sound. The children saw me, screamed, and ran away through the gate of a native village. A village? I was saved! Or was I? I knew from the brochures that there were many native tribes in Hawaii. Some were peaceful, some were warlike. Some were friendly, some unfriendly. Some welcomed strangers, some didn't. Some were helpful, others not that helpful. Some got right to the point while others droned on and on, making the same point over and over.

I decided to take a chance. I hadn't eaten a decent meal in three days, hadn't slept in two, and couldn't remember the last time I had defecated. Soon, I hoped, I would be doing all three.

I didn't want to meet the natives in my tar and feathers. It seemed too casual. So I cleaned up and put on my old clothes. My beret was missing. I saw a monkey wearing it as underpants. It seemed so wrong.

As I approached the village gate, several scowling natives emerged. I walked up with a smile, my arms held wide in friendship, and was hit with a wall of blow darts. When I didn't go down, the natives were puzzled.

The chief stepped forward. He reared back to throw his spear at me. I flashed my medallion at him. It's well known that natives fear the power of the medallion. It worked. He lowered his spear and approached. He was impressed. "This yours?" he said, as he respectfully examined it. I nodded.

# *Patangis*

THE NATIVES called themselves Patangis. The chief told me that in their culture, it was an honor if your parents weren't married, if you were a bastard. Then he asked me if my parents had been married. The whole tribe seemed to lean forward for my response. "No," I said, hoping to provide the right answer, "I'm a bastard." They all broke into convulsive laughter. It was the oldest Patangi joke in the book, but it still worked.

The Patangis said I was a god, and that only gods could climb up palm trees and pick coconuts for them. I insisted that I wasn't a god, but they said oh yes I was.

We went back and forth like that. Finally, I climbed about halfway up a tree trunk and fell off. They seemed to respect that.

I enjoyed my time with the Patangis. The women had no shame about their bodies. Unfortunately, neither did the men.

Like many tribes, they practiced cannibalism, but they weren't in your face about it.

They had a bunch of interesting sayings that I had never heard, like "Red sky at morning, sailor for dinner."

The Patangis had no concept of money. Whenever I would ask them for money, they didn't seem to have any idea what I was talking about.

I tried to show them some of our modern ways, such as how to use a spoon. It's funny how when people are watching you do something you can't do it.

# The Feast

THE PATANGIS threw a big feast in my honor. There were beautiful dancing girls, pounding drums, and a strong drink made from fermented saliva. I was treated to a special batch of fifteen-year-old saliva.

Mount Palinka was spewing lava high into the nighttime sky. It was like a fireworks show, only not as good.

The chief got a little drunk. He started philosophizing. He said the trouble with the world was "Mans not able communicate other mans." He also said the Golden Monkey was overrated.

The featured entertainment consisted of throwing captured prisoners into a pool of electric eels. It might seem barbaric to us, but is it really so different from making a ballerina dance across a stage until she's out of breath?

Next came a stand-up comedian brought in all the way from Honolulu. I felt sorry for him having to follow the electric eels, but he was really funny. He had a big cigar and told jokes about the differences between Patangis and non-Patangis and the differences between men and women. Also he told some political jokes that were pretty edgy. I laughed and laughed.

A little while later I saw his severed head on a stake. What was more upsetting, he had several cigars stuffed in his mouth, even though he had told me earlier he didn't have any more cigars. I looked around, pulled out the cigars, and tucked them inside my shirt.

# Decisions

IT TURNED out to be a surprise party. The surprise was Don and Leilani brought out in cages. When I saw them, the liquor sprayed out of my mouth. The droplets turned into a big fireball as they passed over the campfire. Some natives applauded.

The tribe decided they were going to slowly eat Don, and as guest of honor I was going to be offered the choice pieces. I wanted to tell them there *were* no choice pieces of Don.

I was in a fix. If I didn't eat, I would offend my hosts. But if I ate, and later Don asked me how his foot tasted, I might have to lie and say it was great, even if it wasn't.

Then came an even bigger problem. The natives pulled Leilani from her cage. She knocked a couple of them out cold before they finally got a grip on her. They dragged her to the edge of the precipice. They planned to throw her into the glowing river of lava, as a sacrifice to the volcano. They looked to me for a signal.

What could I do? If I didn't stop the ceremony, the natives would throw Leilani into the lava. But if I did, there would probably be no more drinks or dancing girls. If I saved her, it might rekindle our romance. But if I let them throw her in, it would probably be over between us.

There was a commotion. A beautiful young maiden was fighting with her lover. She screamed at him and, breaking away, ran and jumped off the cliff, into the molten lava below. Her lover wailed and pulled his hair, then ran and jumped as well. This seemed to satisfy everyone, and after a few more drinks we called it a night.

## Adiós, Patangis

By the next morning the volcano had calmed down. Say what you want about human sacrifices, they can't hurt.

The villagers escorted Don and Leilani and me to the gate. The chief pointed at my medallion and said, "What category?"

I waved my hand over one side of it and said, "Abraham Lincoln," then flipped it over and said, "Lesbians." He seemed confused, then laughed. I laughed, too. It's only polite.

I wanted to give the chief a present. But what? That's when I felt the little hula girl in my pocket. I had forgotten all about her! As

I handed it to him I gave her a tap, to show him how it worked. He was speechless.

As we turned to leave, I was hit in the buttock by a blow dart. I playfully pointed *You got me* at the offender. It's fun to leave on a joke.

Walking back to the boat, I got the feeling that Leilani was mad at me for something. I got that feeling because she kept shouting, "You let them kill us!" Also, she kept punching me on the back of the head and kicking me as I tried to crawl away. But the joke was on Leilani. As I wormed my way into the bushes, guess what I found? An arrowhead!

# Dump Leilani

BACK AT the boat, I changed out of my dirty clothes. I put on my tight, skimpy swimsuit and a clean T-shirt, the one that says I'm With Stupid. Also, a fresh underpants beret. I lit up a cigar from the severed head of the comedian. It felt good to be civilized again.

But something was gnawing at my brain. Something was probably gnawing at the comedian's brain, too, but this was different. It occurred to me that I was not making much headway with Leilani. She had not given me pakakka, or even oral pakakka. All of which brought up the question: Let's dump her. Put her in her canoe and tell her to hit the road.

As Leilani loaded the boat, I took Don into the cabin. Leilani could see us through the window, so I turned my head away as I spoke, in case she could read lips like that computer in that outer-space movie.

"Dump Leilani?" said Don. "But she saved both our lives."

*"Once,"* I pointed out.

"And she fixed the engine."

I rolled my eyes. "Don, let's be honest, anyone with a lot of mechanical knowledge could have done that."

"I know where is Gold Monkey," Leilani called out.

"So, you can read lips," I said.

"No read lips. You talk too loud."

"By the way," I corrected, "It's the Gold*en* Monkey. Gold*en*." She glared at me. "Anyway," I said, "what makes you think we're looking for the Golden Monkey?"

"All white men seek gold. That all they want. Their heart sick with greed."

Yes, we want gold, but come on, that's not *all* we want. Our hearts are sick with other things, too.

Don blurted out, "It's true. We came here to steal the Golden Monkey."

And I was the one who had to swear on the Bible?!

Leilani said, "I lead you to Gold Monkey. But cannot take. It forbidden take Gold Monkey. Yes, unnerstand?"

Don and I nodded agreement. Is it wrong to lie because you're planning to steal something? That's a question probably only the philosophers can answer.

One thing I knew for sure: The Golden Monkey did not want to be gawked at. He wanted to be melted down into smooth little ingots and smuggled to America inside someone's rectum.

## A Distant Crash

WE SHOWED Leilani our treasure map. "This map very old," she said. "Not even show Highway 14."

Highway 14? What the heck was Highway 14?!

That's when we heard a huge, roaring crash coming from the direction of the Patangi village. Up on the hillside, all the huts were collapsing, one after another. Patangis were running everywhere, yelling and screaming. The village wall crumpled and fell. Even the giant wooden slingshot, used to fling gripers into the treetops, disintegrated before our eyes.

It was unbelievable! What could have

caused it? I felt that, in a way, I was to blame. If I had let the natives sacrifice Leilani, maybe the gods would have been pleased and this wouldn't have happened.

Don said we should go help them, but Leilani said no, they would kill us.

Maybe just Don could go.

# Devil in a Grass Skirt

WE SAILED on, trying to ignore the big cloud of dust that rose from the native village and the fading screams.

Leilani took the wheel, her grass skirt swaying as she steered this way and that, her coconuts pointing straight ahead, proud and confident.

What was she up to? Was she leading us into a trap? Did she really know the way to the Golden Monkey, or was she just whistling "Dixie"? Would we be trussed up like bales of cotton, then left to die and soon forgotten? She was so gorgeous, but I told myself, Look away, look away.

The river narrowed and sped up. The

engine was straining to move us upstream, as if someone had not fixed it very well. We struggled against the raging foam like a cigarette in a latrine. At last we eased into a rippling pool, fed by a thundering waterfall.

"Looks like a great place to take a shower," I said to Leilani.

"Anyone shower under that, he very stupid," said Leilani.

Man, lighten up, Leilani.

We tied the boat to a crude dock that looked like it had been built by ancient, primitive people, or by the Hawaiian Park Service. Above us loomed Mount Regina, named after Queen Victoria, who was one of England's greatest Reginas.

Leilani pointed up at the rounded, cleft peak, protruding through the sheer white clouds that stretched over it like panties. "Golden Monkey up there," she said.

From here we would go on by foot, or, I was hoping, by piggyback.

# Red Hot Chili Gum

I TRIED to take a shower under the waterfall, hoping Leilani would join me, but I
was knocked unconscious by the force of
the falling water. As I floated facedown, I
was awakened by nipping piranhas.

That night I thought about taking off in
the boat, leaving Don and Leilani stranded.
But I couldn't do it. I didn't know how to
drive the boat. Besides, I deserved the
Golden Monkey. I had worked too hard
for it.

In the morning we packed up the bare
essentials and prepared to "hike" up the
path. I don't know if you've ever been on a

hike before, but it is pure hell. It's mostly walking uphill while you carry things.

I paused to look around. I would miss the old boat. Normally I would laugh at people who became attached to a boat. But now who was laughing? The boat.

Up and up we went. My lungs burned. My legs burned. My mouth burned. I looked at the label on my chewing gum. Red Hot Chili Gum?! When did I buy that?!

I clawed my way through the muck and the mud, on my hands and knees. I was attacked by biting ants. Here's my question: Why are there so many ants, but not that many anteaters? Nice job, Evolution.

I crawled past a lizard. Then the lizard went past me. Then I realized the lizard was just sitting there and I had been sliding downhill.

It felt like I was lying on a giant anvil, being pounded by a giant hammer. I wanted to shout, "I'm flat enough!"

Every cell in my body cried out, and

every cell in my brain hollered back, *Whoa, there, little pardners, let's take 'er easy.* My brain had become a cowboy!

Don took me aside. He said maybe I should get rid of the bottles of scotch in my backpack. I shook my head in disbelief, so hard that my neck burned. "There's no way I'm getting rid of this Glenriddance, Glen," I said, calling Don by his middle name, which he hates. "These scotch bottles are like my children, and I would never abandon my children."

"But you did abandon your children," said Don.

"They weren't my children! They were my niece and nephew! I was only baby-sitting! And I only left them for a little while! Why did they call the police? *Why! Why! Why!*"

Against everything that's holy, I took the last four bottles of Glenriddance from my pack. I kissed each one good-bye and I tossed them down onto the rocks. When

I heard them shatter, I let out a scream of pain and anger and grief. When Don said we could have stashed them somewhere and picked them up on the way back down, I let out an even bigger scream.

# *What Kind of World*

WHAT KIND of a world was this, where people won't help you carry expensive scotch but, oh, they don't mind carrying *water*?

Where a monkey pretends to eat something foul, just to trick you into eating it?

Where heads are shrunken and feet are stunken?

Where even after you explain to people that what you're doing is yodeling, they still want you to stop?

Where a mad scientist can apparently rent a helicopter, no questions asked?

Where plants eat men, and men eat men, but a Patangi won't let you play his drum because you "might hurt it"?

Where you smell a flower and it smells you back?

Where you look and look for your other shoe, and when you finally find it no one seems that happy?

Where people don't mind if you call mosquitoes "skeeters," but they get annoyed if you call them "skits"?

Where you would kill for a hot bath and slaughter everyone in sight for a bubble bath?

Where a raccoon can hypnotize you just by washing his hands?

Where a man weeping in the night is told to "stop cry"?

## What a Fool I'd Been

UP AND up we went, into the clouds. Everything was foggy and slippery and wet, like some kind of dream.

"Mount Regina, she very wet. She always wet," said Leilani. She put her hand on Don's waist.

I had an orgasm in my pants.

Also, I had a realization that made me shudder. How could I have been so stupid? Something was going on between Don and Leilani. Of course! That's why they kept looking at each other when they pitched the tent and cooked the meals and cleaned up afterward. And all the time I had just been sitting there, clueless.

That's why they would go off in the jungle together, and when they came back Leilani would have flowers in her hair and Don would have scrapes on his knees. They seemed to have a certain glow about them— the glow that comes from porking.

Tadpoles of suspicion had been growing in my mind. And now they were full-grown frogs.

That evening Don and Leilani announced they were going off to get some "roughage." They didn't even bother to hide it anymore.

I followed them. I'm good at sneaking up on people if they're having sex. Don laid out a blanket, walking around on his knees to straighten it. Leilani put an orchid behind her ear. They sat down next to each other. Not touching, but close. Every once in a while they would point to a sunlit cloud, or a pair of doves flitting by. Or Leilani would take a leaf from her basket for Don to smell. But mostly they were just talking. And laughing. What in the name of the Pelican God was going on here?

If Don and Leilani weren't having sex, what were they up to? There was only one answer: they were planning to kill me. It all made sense now. It was like looking through out-of-focus binoculars, then throwing the binoculars away and seeing clearly. That way they could cut the Golden Monkey into two pieces instead of three. It would be a lot less work, for one thing.

I knew what I had to do: kill Don. Then, as the victorious bull ape, I would claim Leilani as my mate, if she would be okay with that. Then we would go get the Golden Monkey. After that we would move to Las Vegas.

## Killing Don

IT WOULDN'T be easy to kill Don. I had tried in the past. I would have to come up with the perfect plan. If my plan failed, something told me I would probably never reach the top of Mount Regina. I would meet with some sort of bizarre accident—falling off a cliff or being crushed by a landslide. Or, more likely, Don and Leilani would kill me.

Here are some of the ideas I came up with to do away with Don:

Find an old hand grenade from the war. Then pull the pin, toss it to Don, and say, "Hey, Don, Merry Christmas." But if it didn't blow up, Don might say, "Thanks, but it's not Christmas." So then what would I get him for Christmas?

Put poison mushrooms into Don's meals. (Note: Do not eat the meals yourself *even if they smell delicious*.)

Find some phosphorus; rub in Don's hair. Find some sulfur; rub into Don's hair. Get Don to strike his head across a rough surface.

Find a human skeleton someplace. Tie strings to the bones. Then practice using it as a marionette. Practice and practice, until you can make it tiptoe up behind Don and say, "Oh, Don, it's me, a *SKELETON!*" Oh, yeah, also learn ventriloquism.

Somehow turn Don into a human magnet. (That's as far as I got on that one.)

Find a big rock stuck in the ground. Convince Don we need to move it. Don wrenches his back trying to lift it. We go back home, where he gets hooked on pain pills. He robs a drugstore to get more pain pills, and during the robbery shoots himself in the foot and needs even more pain pills. He overdoses and is rushed to the hospital. On the way, the ambulance is involved in a wreck, and Don wrenches his back even worse. He is able to flag down a cab. The cab driver has back problems, and when he sees Don he thinks Don is making fun of him, and shoots him.

Tell Don, "Hey, Don, how 'bout a glass of orange juice?" But guess what, it's not orange juice. I don't know what it is, but it's not orange juice.

Find a cobra and put it down next to Don. If I can't find a cobra, find a rattlesnake. If no rattlesnake, what about a jack-in-the-box?

Steal a baby gorilla from a gorilla family while wearing a Don mask.

Get Don to eat a big jar of popcorn seeds. Then roast him over a fire.

Find some fireworks that somebody left. Then say, "Hey, Don, let's go shoot off some fireworks." Then go shoot the fireworks. This doesn't really kill Don, but it would be fun.

# The Plan

THE PLAN I finally decided on was complex. But also, in a way, it was simple: I would hit Don over the head with a frying pan.

Some people might say I got this idea from Leilani hitting the turtle man with a frying pan. Listen, Leilani did not invent the idea of hitting someone with a frying pan. That idea has been around a long time. Plus, mine was different—I would hit Don while he was asleep.

I awoke at dawn. That's what no scotch will do for you. I made my way through the dim light to the cooking gear. I couldn't find a frying pan, just one of those whisk things that you stir things with. It would have to do. My plan had come too far.

I tiptoed up to the snoozing Don and raised my weapon. But I noticed something. It was a dimple on his neck, from when I shot him with a BB gun when we were kids. I raised the whisk again, but something else caught my eye. Between his fingers was the old cigarette burn, from when we were teenagers and I taught Don how to smoke.

I rolled him over so I wouldn't have to look at him when I hit him. That's when I saw the surgical scar on his back, from when he gave me one of his kidneys.

I couldn't do it. We'd had too many fun times together. Also, what if I ever needed his other kidney?

I tossed the whisk to the ground. It bounced over and hit Don on the head. He woke up, looked at me then at the whisk, and said, "Hey! You were trying to kill me! Again!"

I turned and started to run, but Don

caught me and tripped me. I fell to the ground, hard. I got up and tripped him. Then he tripped me back. "I give up, I give up!" I said, lying there. I tried to yank him off his feet, but he blocked my hand with his tripping foot.

"Stop!" yelled Leilani.

While he was distracted, I tied Don's shoelaces together. I got up and motioned him toward me. "Come on, let's see what you got." He fell flat on his face. I started laughing, until I felt a tap on my shoulder. It was Don. He double-tripped me.

"Stop fight!" said Leilani. "There is Golden Monkey!"

We looked up. The clouds had parted. There before us, in the gathering light, was the Cave of the Golden Monkey.

# The Cave of the Golden Monkey

WE SPRINTED up the ancient path. Finally, Don and I would get what we so richly deserved.

"No need run!" Leilani called after us.

We entered the yawning mouth of the cave. A bat fluttered overhead. And there before us, illuminated by some mysterious force, was the object of our quest. "There it is, the Golden Monkey!" I gasped. I had the urge to throw myself down and worship it, but I resisted. Instead I yelled, "We found it! We found it!" I jumped up and down and hugged Don and Leilani. I wanted that monkey so bad I was drooling, even more than normal.

The Golden Monkey was sitting cross-legged on a rough stone altar. It wasn't as big as I thought it would be. Still, it was all ours.

Don didn't seem that happy. He was rubbing his face and whimpering. But I was already trying to figure out how we could get the thing down the mountain. I whispered to Don, "Let's make Leilani carry it."

Something was wrong. Don had a sick look on his face. I heard voices. I noticed a young couple with a stroller off to one side. They were taking a photo. I saw an older woman listening to an audio guide. Just coming into the cave was a tour group. I picked up a rock to throw at them. Don stopped me. "We screwed up," he said. "The Golden Monkey was found long ago. It's a...tourist attraction."

*"Huh?"*

"That's why the old crone gave us the map. She just thought we'd enjoy seeing it."

*"Huh?! Huh?! Huh?!"* I couldn't believe it. I turned to Leilani. *"Why didn't you tell us this?!"*

"I say to you, 'Cannot take Gold Monkey.'"

*"Yeah, but you weren't very clear as to why!"*

For once she softened. "I not want Don leave me."

Don and Leilani gazed into each other's eyes, and kissed. "Maybe it worked out for the best," said Don, looking at the Golden Monkey and smiling a stupid, self-satisfied smile.

Don and Leilani held hands and walked out of the cave together. God, love is sickening.

## You'd Do the Same

I NOTICED it wasn't a bat flying around but a boomerang some kid was throwing. It almost hit me in the head.

I moved closer to the Golden Monkey to get a better look. The mysterious force illuminating it turned out to be spotlights.

"Please stand back, sir," said a guard.

I saw that the Golden Monkey wasn't even solid gold. It was only clay, painted gold. And a lot of the gold had peeled off. Plus it had disturbingly prominent genitalia. I don't like glaring genitalia on statues, especially monkey statues.

"Sir, please step back. This statue is extremely valuable. It's worth more money than you have, or that you'll ever have." It seemed like an odd thing for a guard to say. But he was right. Yet I did have one thing, something you can't put a value on. And that was the rock in my hand.

Sometimes, in rare moments, your thoughts and emotions and desires crystallize into pure thoughtlessness. The Eastern swamis can achieve this, and so can some checkout clerks. And as I gazed down at the rock, that's what happened to me.

I backed up several steps, and with a running start hurled the rock at the Golden Monkey. The statue shattered. The crowd was shocked into silence.

Inside the rubble was something bright gold. I reached in and grabbed it. It was a smaller Golden Monkey. It was heavy. I turned and ran.

As I ran, I said a little prayer to the Pelican God that I would make it out alive, and that I would be able to kill anyone who tried to stop me.

## *Diversions*

WHY IS there always some jerk in every crowd who yells, "Get him!"

The mob of tourists was hot on my heels, screaming and howling things like "He's got the Golden Monkey!" and "Stop him!" They didn't even know there *was* a real golden monkey until I discovered it. Now, all of a sudden, it belongs to them. Sometimes when you run away you don't know whether to laugh or cry.

I raced from the cave, down the wheel-chair ramp and across the parking lot, almost getting hit by a tour bus with a destination sign that said "Golden Monkey." I pounded on the door of a bus marked

"Honolulu" that was pulling out, but the driver ignored me. I had to think of something fast. I pulled out my ChapStick. I tossed it toward the angry mob and hid behind a parked car.

The crowd gathered round the Chap-Stick, stared at it, then began fighting over it. It was a brutal fistfight. Finally one man emerged triumphant. He pulled off the cap and smeared the soothing balm thickly on his lips as a taunt to the others. Then he laughed and threw the rest of the ChapStick away.

I have been in many mobs, and the truth is, the average mob has a hard time remembering what it was doing. To keep them distracted, I threw my wallet out. They tore it to bits. One man got my driver's license. "Yahoo!" he shouted, holding it up. He ran over to a car that was idling, pulled the driver out, and sped away.

"I got his library card!" yelled another man. I didn't even know I had a library card. He ran off, I guess to check out a book.

I tried to duckwalk away, but the Golden Monkey's hand got caught on a hubcap and pulled it off. The hubcap went rolling around and around in a big circle. The tourists watched it and took photos as the circles got smaller and smaller. I watched, too. I probably should have slipped away, but you can't help wondering how long it can keep rolling like that.

"There he is! Get him!" yelled a man standing next to me, right in my ear.

I jerked loose and ran past the edge of the parking lot, into the dense rain forest.

The mob came charging after me. But now they were in my element, the jungle. The odds were shifting in my favor.

# Vines

I GOT tangled up in some vines. I don't know how. Where do these stupid vines come from anyway?!

The mob spread out, looking for me. Many were now carrying pitchforks. What kind of gift shop sells pitchforks?!

I lay perfectly still. I would appear as just a clump of vines, or maybe a dummy that someone had thrown away and now vines were growing all over it.

"Here's his beret," someone said, holding up my underpants. "He's around here somewhere."

A bug crawled next to my face. It was a Hawaiian black pepper bug. If he sprayed his pepperish spray, I would sneeze and give myself away.

Slowly, deliberately, I reached in my pocket and pulled out the box with Bizzy's nose plugs. I dumped the nose plugs out, grabbed the bug, and stuck him in the box. And slipped the box back in my pocket.

Two men approached, stabbing the bushes with their pitchforks. They were so close I could hear them talking.

"We shouldn't have fallen for that Chap-Stick trick," said one.

"Maybe not," said the other. "But we shouldn't beat ourselves up over it."

With that, they began beating each other up. The mob gathered round. I couldn't tell which one they were rooting for, the one who said they shouldn't have fallen for the trick or the one who said they shouldn't blame themselves. I guess it doesn't really matter.

While they were sidetracked, I loosened the vines and slunk away. I thought I'd made it when I heard "There he is! Get him!"

# The Coconut

EVEN THOUGH I was still dragging some vines, and even though the Golden Monkey was getting heavier and heavier, and even though my lips were in desperate need of moisturizing balm, I ran on. It's amazing how you can push yourself when you're in the right.

As I ran, I heard one tourist shout that he'd seen me earlier but thought I was a dummy. That made me feel good.

The mob reached what I call the second stage of mobdom. That's where you don't yell so much but you chase harder. And soon they were right behind me.

As I was looking back I ran headfirst

into a tree trunk. A coconut fell and hit the lead pursuer on the head, knocking him unconscious.

The coconut shot over and hit another man on the forehead, then ricocheted into a big spiderweb. The web flung the coconut into the face of an old woman. She shrieked in pain.

The coconut rolled into a gopher hole. A heavyset man went over and looked in. The coconut shot up, *ka-ping*ed off his skull and hit another man right on the tailbone. *"AGGGHHH! MY COCCYX!"* he wailed, arching his back.

The coconut bounced into a geyser. The geyser erupted, firing the coconut high in the air. The tourists all watched it. It came down and smashed the finger of a man who was pointing up at it.

As I sneaked away, I looked back to see the mob stabbing the coconut with their pitchforks.

# The Skeleton

I STUMBLED on. I crashed through some undergrowth, down into a dark hollow in the ground. I got the feeling I was not alone. I flicked my lighter. Right beside me was a *SKELETON!* (I hope you weren't drinking anything when you read that last sentence.)

I quickly scooted backwards. It was the skeleton of a Japanese soldier from the war. He was still wearing his uniform, still manning his machine gun after all these years. My shock gave way to sympathy. Brave, loyal soldier, I thought. I patted him on his shoulder. His machine gun started firing. I heard screams of panic. The mob was right in front of us, and the bullets were tearing into them. So many tourists, in the prime of their tourism, were cut down.

Some people say I should have stopped the machine gun. But here's my thinking: by the time you're a skeleton, you pretty much have a right to do what you want.

The machine gun fell silent. And soon I fell asleep. There's something about the cool darkness of a machine gun nest, with the wind whistling through the nose hole of a skeleton, that really makes you drowsy.

I was awakened by the roar of an engine, followed by a strange squeaking and clanking. I peeked out. My jaw dropped. I turned to the skeleton. His jaw had fallen off. An old battle tank from the war was coming straight for us!

I started to climb out and run, but the tank's machine guns opened up on us. I scrambled back into the shelter. I patted the skeleton, and he began firing back. The tank kept rumbling toward us. Our bullets bounced off the thick metal. The tank meant to turn us into two crushed skeletons, one with meat, one without.

I saw that my bony friend had a couple of hand grenades attached to his belt. I pulled one off. The tank was so old it had big rust holes in it. I chucked the grenade toward one. It bounced off and exploded.

The tank kept coming. I pulled the pin on the second grenade. The skeleton seemed to give me a look that said, *You can do it.* I leaned out and pitched the grenade underhand, straight into a rust hole. The hatch opened up and two tourists jumped out and ran. With a tremendous blast, the tank blew apart.

I turned to the skeleton to celebrate. But something was wrong. He was bleeding.

The rest of the mob came out from hiding. Without a word they assembled, surrounding us. Their gaze was squinty and intense. They had reached the third level of mobdom. No more distractions. No more rushing this way to stab something or that way to burn something down. They were now a mature mob. In a way, I was proud of them.

I looked over at the skeleton. He had only a few bullets left. And he was growing weaker.

The mob started clacking their pitchforks together in unison. They began marching toward us, still clacking. I was faced with mankind's two great choices: begging for mercy or digging into the ground.

*Clack, clack, clack!*

I thought of another choice. I could toss them the Golden Monkey. But not the *whole* monkey. They didn't deserve that. I began hitting the Golden Monkey against a rock, trying to knock his head off.

*Clack, clack, clack!*

I banged harder and harder. They were right on top of us.

*CLACK, CLACK, CLACK!*

That's when I heard a mournful noise in the distance. The tourists heard it, too. They stopped and listened, tilting their heads. It was honking, the honking of tour bus drivers. They were signaling to their passengers. It was time to head back.

The tourists could not resist. Like zombies, they turned and trudged off toward the honking.

# The Tracking Device

As I was debating whether I should wave good-bye to the tourists, I sensed something behind me. I turned. You know how when you don't instantly recognize someone you sort of hem and haw? "Well, hello there, uh, uh..."

"Doctor Ponzari."

It was Doctor Ponzari! A bolt of lightning exploded overhead, so close both of us ducked.

Doctor Ponzari looked different. His face was hideously burned and disfigured. He had only a few sprigs of hair left, and pieces of helicopter were sticking out of his scalp. He wore wraparound sunglasses. His suit, what was left of it, was charred black. It seemed like smoke was still rising from him. To be honest, it was a pretty cool look.

He pointed a revolver at me. Everything I hated about Doctor Ponzari came rushing back. How, when we were at his house, I had asked him if he had any guns or hand grenades, and he said, "No, this a place of peace." Oh, but he can get a gun when *he* wants one. Also how he kept asking me to please stop tapping on his aquarium.

"You're probably wondering how I found you, Mister Slurps."

I wasn't, but I said yes anyway.

"Someone implanted a tracking device in one of your teeth." He waited for me to say something, but I couldn't think of anything. After an awkward moment, he cleared his throat and continued: "You have refused to help me file an insurance claim, and that is your prerogative. But I will not allow you to steal one of the great treasures of Hawaii."

I raised my eyebrows and nodded toward

the Golden Monkey. "Yes, the Golden Monkey," he sighed impatiently. He said the Golden Monkey must be saved for future generations. As soon as I heard "future generations," I stopped listening. But I started listening again when I heard "tits."

"The Golden Monkey should be available to everyone, from senior citizens on down to little tots." Oh, *tots*.

I flashed my medallion at him, but he showed no fear. In fact, he seemed annoyed. He grabbed it roughly from me. "My Nobel Prize! I wondered where that went." He put it around his neck, and told me to hand him the Golden Monkey. I hesitated.

"Don't make me use this, Mister Slurps." After seeing the expression on my face, he added, "Yes, the gun." He said he was an excellent marksman.

Out of the corner of my eye I noticed that the machine gun was slowly turning toward Ponzari. Was it the wind? Was it ants? Or was Bony trying to help me? Science says you shouldn't give human qualities to skeletons, but sometimes I wonder.

I tried to keep Doctor Ponzari distracted. "I like your hairdo," I said.

Doctor Ponzari wheeled and fired a single shot at the skeleton. Bony slumped over his machine gun. I saw my opening. I ran.

Ponzari fired at me. The bullet knocked off my glasses. Another shot cut my belt in half so that my pants fell around my ankles. I shuffled on.

"I don't want to hurt you," he shouted after me.

He fired again. A big bunch of bananas fell and knocked me to the ground. After I gathered my wits, I yelled, "Ha, ha, you missed again! You hit these bananas instead!"

I came to the edge of a cliff and almost fell over. I knocked off a few rocks. It took them so long to hit the bottom I thought they were playing a joke on me. I felt woozy. I staggered backward and dropped the Golden Monkey in the mud.

As Doctor Ponzari came slowly walking up, I noticed something else. Emerging from the trees were several fierce-looking turtle men, each holding several long, pointed sticks. With them were the two baby turtle men.

"Don't look now, but there are turtle men behind you with sticks," I said.

"Please, Mister Slurps, that's the oldest line in the book."

The turtle men let out a horrible hissing noise. Doctor Ponzari turned. The two baby turtle men were pointing at him. Ponzari looked at me, then at the gold medallion on his chest. "It wasn't me!" he implored them. "It was *him!*" He pulled off the medallion and threw it to the ground. I dove for cover. A hail of sharp sticks stuck in his chest. *"AAAAAGHHHHHEE!"* he screamed, dropping his gun. He twisted, just in time to get another volley of sticks in the back, then twisted again to get some more in the front. He lurched back and forth. A couple of late sticks bounced off his head. He looked like a porcupine, only not a regular porcupine—a porcupine of sticks.

He picked up the Golden Monkey. Just as he did, a bolt of lightning shot from the clouds and hit the monkey. Ponzari was jolted backward. When he got up, his sticks were on fire.

He stood there for a second, then staggered to the cliff and keeled over, into the abyss. On the way down, he was hit again by lightning. He disappeared through the mist. I heard a heavy thud, a pause, another thud, then a splat.

I know this sounds crazy, but in a way I felt sorry for him. Maybe he was evil, but without evil people in the world, how could there be people like me?

# The Airplane

A SMALL airplane buzzed by at cliff level. I stayed down. I heard a voice in my tooth. It was as if there was a little speaker in there. "This is Uncle Lou," said the voice. I looked around. "I'm in the airplane," said the voice. "The one that's flying by you right now. Yes, that one." It was Uncle Lou! For once I was happy to see him. Especially since it was starting to sprinkle.

I picked up my medallion and put it around my neck. Poor little medallion, he'd been through a lot.

I picked up the Golden Monkey. He'd been through a lot, too.

I pulled up my pants. They'd also been through a lot.

I picked up Doctor Ponzari's gun and vowed that it would never again be used for evil.

I pulled up my pants once more and vowed that they would never again be used for evil, either.

I picked up my glasses and vowed to get some new ones. Maybe with frames made from turtle-man shell.

Uncle Lou landed on the fairway of a golf course right nearby. He pulled onto the green and spun around, ready to take off again. His tires made deep ruts in the short, smooth grass.

I ran out to greet him. I was so happy I hugged him and fired my new gun into the air.

"Don't fire the gun," he said.

"Okay," I said.

I showed him the Golden Monkey. His eyes opened wide. "You did it! I knew you could." He blew cigar smoke in my face. "At last, you're a man."

I started blubbering.

# Highway 14

I HELD on tight to the Golden Monkey as I climbed into the plane. Too many had sacrificed their lives so that I might have it, and later sell it.

As we took off, three golfers ran toward the plane, shaking their fists. Uncle Lou didn't slow down. One golfer couldn't get out of the way in time, and the propeller cut off his arm. I have to admit, I laughed at the time. But now when I think about it I just chuckle.

The plane banked toward Honolulu. I saw Highway 14 below. It looked like it was only a few miles to town. Off to the right, the mighty Paloonga River twisted and turned a hundred times to reach the same spot.

"You took the long way," said Uncle Lou.

He told me to put on my parachute. "I'll hold on to the Golden Monkey while you do." I started to hand it to him, but something made me hesitate. Screwball was sitting on the parachute, growling. Uncle Lou shooed him off and took the Golden Monkey from me.

As soon as I had the parachute on, Uncle Lou reached across and opened my door. And pushed me out.

If you've never used a parachute before, trust me, you will grab at anything that feels like it might be a latch or a handle or a zipper that will get the thing open. And just as you start biting at it, whatever you did before finally opens it and the parachute almost pulls your teeth out.

I floated down near Honolulu. I tried to land with one of those running landings that skydivers do, but I tripped and got tangled up in the parachute strings. What do they need so many strings for, anyway?!

I got arrested. They questioned me about the Golden Monkey, but all I told them was that Uncle Lou had it, and what he looked like, and what his plane looked like, and that his dog was vicious and would probably have to be shot.

I was sentenced to six months of community service. The service was to stay in jail. I plotted an escape. The key to my plan would focus on one central element: waiting until the guard left, and then, before he got back, escaping. For complicated reasons, the escape never worked out.

Uncle Lou made it back to America with the Golden Monkey. Hawaii requested that it be sent back, but Uncle Lou told them to perform oral sex on him.

Am I angry that Uncle Lou stole the Golden Monkey from me? Of course I am—what kind of a question is that?

I thought about going back and stealing the Golden Monkey from Uncle Lou, or at least vandalizing his house. But every time I mentioned this idea to anyone I got an electric shock in my tooth. At least I got to keep the Nobel Prize and the gun. And really, what else do you need in life?

In case you're worried about the black pepper bug, don't be. I released him in Honolulu. The town never had black pepper bugs before, but then, for some reason, it was swarming with them.

# The Wedding

DOCTOR PONZARI survived the sharp sticks and the fall, although he spent nearly a week in the hospital. I billed him for my belt and my new glasses. Don and Leilani went to work for him, developing medicines from leaves. Great, that's all we need, more medicines. Maybe one day Doctor Ponzari will turn his jungle estate into a place for good. Maybe a carnival. With a sideshow of freaks.

Leilani said she would give me pekoocha if I would sign the stupid insurance paper Doctor Ponzari kept waving at me. I signed. But it turned out pekoocha is just a kiss on the cheek. It sounds a lot better than that, doesn't it?

Bizzy became head of the Tourist Board. It was he who came up with the idea of adding an extra "i" to *Hawaii*, so it's now *Hawaiii*.

Don and Leilani got married. Leilani was radiant in her skirt of rarest ivory grass and her bra made from two albino starfish. And Don didn't look like the total jerk he is. At the ceremony Leilani did a hula dance that made my little statuette look like a stupid souvenir on a spring.

## Picking Up the Pieces

I DECIDED to stay in Hawaiii. It was Pingle free, for one thing. I got an apartment down in Appliance Town and started my own business. It was a boardwalk booth where you paid to shoot me with a blow dart. If you didn't believe it was real poison, you could shoot a bum that I hired. Some people said the bum was just faking it, but you can't fake convulsions like that. The only catch was I had to keep changing bums before they got used to the poison, too.

I was making good money. And there were the little rewards. You never forget the look on a child's face the first time he hits you with a blow dart. "I got him!" they squeal.

I continued to practice Pelicanism, but it was a less strict form of Pelicanism. I even made some headway on my novel, *Muscular Angry Clown*. I got to the part where the other clowns accuse him of using steroids and he gives them all karate chops.

Then my whole world came crashing down.

## It All Falls Apart

THE CHIEF of the Patangis was sitting on the edge of my bed when I came in. He held up my little stenchite hula girl and began shouting angrily at me. He raised his spear. I flashed my medallion at him, but he threw the spear anyway. It stuck in the door as I dove out.

The chief dragged me back inside. He began pounding my head against the radiator. I know what you're thinking: a radiator in Honolulu? Look, don't worry about that right now. The main thing is, I was getting killed.

Every head bang brought me closer to unconsciousness. And jolted the hula girl closer and closer to the edge of the bed. Would she be the last thing I ever saw? One final, tremendous head slam sent her tumbling onto the wooden floor. The building began to tremble. Everything was cracking and splitting apart, plaster falling, pictures on the wall tilting so they weren't lined up straight anymore. I broke free and stumbled out into the street. People were screaming and tripping as they fled in all directions. Building after building collapsed, like dominoes. Big pieces of debris were flipped into the air, like tiddlywinks. The noise was tremendous, like shaking dice in a giant Yahtzee cup.

As I ran, I tried to help out where I could. I helped an old man in a wheelchair get out of my way and into a ditch, where he'd be safe. I helped some people carry some things out of a store. I led a group of young nurses into a dark culvert, where we huddled together for safety. Finally the noise stopped. The whole of Honolulu lay in ruins, as it does to this day. What had caused it? An earthquake? Gophers? The wrath of the Pelican God?

The saddest thing for me was that my lovely hula girl was now buried under rubble. She deserved better. She should be sitting on a wooden mantel at the White House. Or on the throne of England.

# The Death of Uncle Lou

I DECIDED to leave Honolulu. There was nothing left for me there. I moved over to Diarroa, which turned out to be a shithole.

Will I ever get back to America? Will the Golden Monkey ever be returned to Hawaiii? Will I ever find true love? These are questions that only the writer of this book can answer, and I cannot.

I was pondering this when a messenger arrived with a package. The monkey who lives in the garden jumped into the open window, thinking it might be food. But it wasn't. It was a letter saying that Uncle Lou had died. His body had rejected his new Tomlin. The note said he had left something for me in his will. Which was in the package.

I couldn't help feeling sad at Uncle Lou's death, yet also pleased that all those dinners at his house were finally going to pay off. I opened the package, and there was one of Uncle Lou's old boxing gloves. *Huh?!* A button said "Press Here." I did. The boxing glove shot up on the end of a spring and knocked me out.

When I woke up, the monkey was chewing on my glasses.

# *Acknowledgments*

Thanks, most especially, to my wife, Marta Chavez Handey, for her tireless help with this project. Many thanks also to Bill Novak, George Meyer, Kit Boss, Maria Semple, Chris Hart, Max Pross, Tom Gammill, T. Sean Shannon, and Lev Novak.

Thanks, too, to my editor, Ben Greenberg, and my agent, Jin Auh.

Apologies to the people of Honolulu.

## About the Author

JACK HANDEY is the author of the "Deep Thoughts" series of humor books. He lives in New Mexico.